W9-AKC-773

Donated to
SAINT PAUL PUBLIC LIBRARY

A FAMILY TRAIT

Terri Martin

Holiday House/New York

To those wild, wonderful, and wacky women
of the best-ever critique group: Bonnie Alkema, Ardyce Czuchna-Curl,
Betty Horvath, Carol Fenner, Wendy Risk, and former member
Ellen Howard, for manufacturing the glue
to make me stick to this.

And to my editor, Mary Cash, for the perpetual hand-holding.

And to my boss, Sid Durham, for giving me the time.

And to my husband, Wayne, for believing in me.

And to my parents for giving me the childhood
that was so much a part of this book.

Copyright © 1999 by Terri Martin
ALL RIGHTS RESERVED
Printed in the United States of America
FIRST EDITION

Library of Congress Cataloging–in–Publication Data

Martin, Terri.
A family trait / Terri Martin. – 1st ed.
p.   cm.
Summary: Living with her mother and grandparents on their Michigan
farm, eleven–year–old Iris tries to find out about her father, who
died before she was born, and to solve a local murder mystery
involving a friend of her grandmother.
ISBN 0–8234–1467–1
[1. Mystery and detective stories.   2. Farm life–Michigan–
Fiction.   3. Grandparents–Fiction.   4. Michigan–Fiction.]
I. Title.
PZ7.M36423Fam   1999   99–17867
[Fic]–dc21   CIP

Chapter One

I spent near five minutes running my finger up and down the page in my *American College Dictionary*, looking for the word that Alice Pruitt had spat out at me like a bad peanut. I found the word on the same page as a lot of other words starting with "ill": illegal, ill-fated, ill-gotten, illicit. When I sounded out the word, *illegitimate*, there was no question that it was the same word that Alice had used.

I had told Alice that I would eat worms and die before I'd tell her where the Voodoo Shack was hidden deep in Hazard Swamp. That was our club pact. We had all sworn to eat worms and die if we broke any of the club rules. Luckily, the only rule so far was to keep the whereabouts of the Voodoo Shack secret, and none of us was just dying to tell Alice Pruitt how to find it.

When I had recited this pact, Alice put her hands on her hips and stuck her nose in the air so high she liked to give herself a nosebleed.

"Who wants to join your ol' club anyway?" she had said in a voice that reminded me of chalk taking a bad turn on the blackboard. "Besides, I'm thinking of forming a club of my own, and it won't include ... your kind."

What did she mean, my kind?

"The membership of my club will be restricted to those who can trace their lineage back several generations. Mother is helping me with a list. It certainly won't include any kids from trashy families, or–"

"Who are you calling trashy!" I yelled, giving Alice a small shove.

"And it won't help to resort to violence, Iris Weston– I guess that name will just have to do, since you don't *have* a father. Well, that's not exactly true. Everyone has a father, it's just that those who will be in my club will know who theirs is."

"That so?" I snorted.

"Yes, Iris, that's so. Mother says that you're illegitimate, and should therefore be disqualified from my membership roster."

I knew it was a name–calling word–*illegitimate*. Alice was not about to call me something nice, and just the sound of it had a bad ring to it. Course, she was just ticked off because I wouldn't tell her where the Voodoo Shack was. But I didn't like the notion that Alice Pruitt's mother was discussing my–what was that word?–lineage.

"And you're a sissy–pants," I had zinged back at her. I couldn't think up any great comebacks.

I hadn't given Alice's hissy fit much thought until I was sitting at the kitchen table trying to do my homework. Usually I had better things to do than hunt up words in the dictionary, but I happened to have it right with me to help decipher *Silas Marner*, the book my sixth-grade class had been assigned to read. Besides, I figured I might be able to store up the word for use at a later time.

The definition said it meant *not legitimate*. Well, that's like saying unhappy is "not happy." But it went on to say some other pretty harsh things. *Unlawful*. I knew what that meant. Crossing the street against the traffic light is unlawful. I admit to it, but I always look both ways. *Illegal*. More of the same against-the-law-type stuff. Maybe Alice Pruitt saw me jaywalking. My finger came to an abrupt halt at the next part of the definition. *Born out of wedlock; an illegitimate child*. I strongly suspected that this is what Alice meant, or at least what her mother meant, when she'd told Alice this word.

But what did it mean, born out of wedlock? What was a wedlock? Maybe I wasn't born in a hospital. Maybe they forgot to lock something. I turned the pages of the dictionary to the *W* section. *Wedlock: state of marriage; matrimony*. Born out of– Momma and my father not married? I slammed the dictionary closed with such a bang that my pencil jumped right off the kitchen table onto the floor and rolled under the refrigerator.

It was a big fat lie. Alice Pruitt's mother was spreading lies, like everybody says she does. I wish Deputy Skinner could arrest folks for telling lies.

I was sure my momma was married to my father. I never knew him, my father. Whenever I asked questions about him, Momma's lower lip would start to tremble and Gran would give me a harsh look, like I was asking something bad. Gramps had told me that my father was killed in the Korean War, where Momma had met him when she was over there as a nurse.

"What was that racket?"

I near jumped out of my skin. Gran has a way of just appearing out of nowhere and scaring the daylights out of folks.

"I asked you a question, Young Lady."

I bought a little time by going over to the refrigerator and crawling around to fetch my pencil that had settled next to the drip pan. I could see Gran out of the corner of my eye, her foot tapping. She reached up and pushed a strand of loose hair back into her bun. If that hair knew what was good for it, it would stay put.

I slid back into my chair and wiped the lint off my pencil before I commenced to chew on it. "What racket, Gran? I'm just sitting here doing my homework. I dropped my pencil, is all."

She walked up to me and got close enough so's I could smell the lemon Pledge on her. I knew she wasn't buying it, doing my homework, since the sheet of paper in front of me was blank, except for a doodle in the corner. I was supposed to be working on my book report for *Silas Marner*. I hadn't really read the book and had been planning to skim it and crank out the assigned four pages just as soon as I finished looking up *illegitimate*.

"Sounded like a gunshot, way you're slamming things around here. You know your momma worked the late shift at the hospital. She's got to get her rest. How's she supposed to do that with you throwing books around?"

I shrugged my shoulders. I had learned not to argue with Gran, from the day Momma and I came to live with her and Gramps on the farm. That had been when I was just seven years old. Momma had pulled me right out of my second-grade class one day. She was a nurse in the emergency room of Henry Ford Hospital in Detroit, Michigan, where folks came in all shot up and stabbed or sick from drugs or liquor. Momma said it was worse than the war sometimes. She finally got just plain fed up, said the city was no place to raise a child. I remember her sitting at the table, scribbling on a pad of paper, then wadding up the pages and throwing them away. I found out she was trying to write to Gran and Gramps, but was having an awful time getting the words down. I guess Momma and Gran had had harsh words when I was just a baby, and things had been bad ever since. I had smoothed out one of the crumpled sheets and read it. Momma was asking Gran and Gramps if they could patch things up and for us to go live with them on their farm.

It was driving me crazy, watching Momma try again and again to write that letter, then throw it away. So, when I was writing my thank-you note for my birthday money–Gran and Gramps always sent me a real nice card with money tucked inside–I put it down plain and simple. Momma thought that we should go live with them, and that was that. About a week later, Momma yanked me out of school, already had the station wagon packed, and off we headed for Scottsburg, Michigan. I remember her hands shook so bad I was afraid she couldn't hang on to the steering wheel. "We're going home, baby," she said, her voice all quivery.

So that's how I came to find myself sitting at the kitchen table with Gran looking over me like a prison warden. I figured I'd keep my mouth shut for the time being about this *illegitimate* business, just like I didn't ask anything about the pictures that I had taken a peek at in Momma's nursing books. My favorite section was Human Reproduction. There was some interesting stuff there. I was trying to work up the nerve to sneak the book out and take it to the clubhouse for review at one of the meetings.

"Don't sass me," said Gran as she moved over to the kitchen counter and pulled open a cupboard.

You couldn't win with Gran. Even a shoulder shrug was considered sass.

"I'll fix you a can of Franco–American spaghetti for lunch, then I want to see some words written on that school paper," she said as she began twisting the can opener with her crooked fingers.

"Want me to open that for you, Gran?"

"No, child, I'm not a cripple. I guess I can open a can of spaghetti."

"Why don't you get an electric can opener?"

"Why don't you start writing about that book. You read it, didn't you?"

I began to work on the eraser with my teeth. I tried to think of an answer that wouldn't be a lie and wouldn't incriminate me. I finally mumbled some nonsense into my pencil eraser. Even though I didn't really say anything, Gran somehow knew the answer to her own question.

"Do you want to be held back in the sixth grade?" Gran asked me. She asked me that a lot. I wasn't expected to answer, since it was really more of a threat than a question. The whole trick with Gran was to know when you were expected to speak and when you were expected to be quiet like you were mulling over ways to wash away your sins. I hoped I wouldn't be flunked out of the sixth grade just because I hadn't read *Silas Marner*. I had tried to read it, I really had, I just couldn't make it through the first chapter. I had no trouble with my Nancy Drew mysteries. *Silas Marner* was different.

I buried my nose in the book for a moment, trying to look interested.

In that far-off time superstition clung easily round every person or thing that was all unwonted, or even intermittent and occasional merely, like the visits of the peddler or the knife-grinder. No one knew where wandering men had their homes or their origin; and how was a man to be explained unless you at least knew somebody who knew his father and mother?

That phrase caught me like a fly in a spiderweb: *and how was a man to be explained unless you at least knew somebody who knew his father and mother?* I supposed the question applied to girls as well as men. Course everybody knew my momma and Gran and Gramps. But what about my father? Everybody got all tight-lipped when I asked questions about him, then they'd send me to my room to do my homework or outside to clean the chicken coop. I learned real quick to avoid the subject, though there was a spot inside me that ached when I thought about it.

I heard Gran stirring my spaghetti. She poured a glass of milk and plunked it down next to me. She bent over, looking at the book, smoothing back my tangled hair.

"Humpf," she said, then went back to dish up my lunch.

Like I said, you had to learn how to read my gran. Pushing my hair back like that and the "humpf" were signs of softening. I suppose the "humpf" was her opinion of the book, or maybe she noticed that I had forgotten to brush my hair. Since I was afraid to ask about my father, I decided to investigate the situation by the indirect route.

"Gran, what's 'illegitimate' mean?"

I could tell that hit her like a bolt out of the blue. She almost dropped my plate of Franco-American in front of me. That strand of hair popped out of her bun like a coil spring. I became very interested in my spaghetti, and tried to see how much I could twist around my fork.

"Iris Mae Weston, where in tarnation did you hear that word?"

There was only one thing worse than being called Young Lady by Gran, and that was being called by my full Christian name of Iris Mae Weston. Gran seemed to enjoy using my name more than I enjoyed hearing it, though even she admitted it didn't fit me too well. She allowed that it was her idea, the name Iris, after her sister who died when she was a baby. Momma says she hopes I'll grow into the name. She says right now I'm at the bulb stage, before the green starts to show. After the green comes the bloom. Momma says she reckons the bloom will come in a few years, maybe in about the eighth or ninth grade. I was thinking, while I felt Gran's eyes burning into me, that I wished I was a bulb so's I would be buried deep in the dirt.

When the name Iris is put with my middle name, Mae–which everybody always spells wrong–and my last name, Weston, I know I might be chewing on a bitter old piece of Ivory soap.

"I'm waiting," said Gran, that foot doing its tap dance again.

If I told her that Alice Pruitt had repeated the word to me, then I would be blowing soap bubbles for sure. I don't know why the mouth gets all the blame. Seems to me the eyes, ears, and brain play a part in picking up words and sinful acts they shouldn't be seeing, hearing, or remembering. I guess folks can't figure out a way to wash away an evil until it gets to the mouth.

Nope, I couldn't tell her that Alice Pruitt had name-called me that word, much as I would have liked to. But if I told Gran that I'd read it in a dictionary, then the word found its way into my mouth in an acceptable manner. Gran couldn't accuse me of wrongdoing any more than if I had stumbled across the part about begotten sons and daughters in the Bible, as opposed to, say, a nursing medical book. And it wasn't a lie.

"Dictionary," I said, tapping my pencil on the tattered cover of the book.

Gran sniffed, like she smelled something overripe. "Well, then, Miss, I guess you *know* what it means if you looked it up."

Miss was another one of my names. My degree of sin had been downgraded from Iris Mae Weston to Miss, which meant, though on thin ice, I was okay if I walked carefully.

I sucked in a spaghetti noodle through my lips. I felt some sauce dribble down my chin.

"I've seen pigs at the trough with more table manners," said Gran, tossing me a napkin. I wiped my chin and hunched over my plate. There was no end to my disgraceful behavior. It was a sure thing that Gran despised bad table manners more than the taint of a bad word. I could feel the thin ice crack under my feet.

I rose from the table and carried my dishes to the sink and turned on the faucet. I could feel Gran's eyes on me. She was suspicious probably because I never voluntarily did dishes.

After I carefully wiped my plate, silverware, and glass and put them away in the cupboard, I picked up *Silas Marner.*

"I'm going to finish reading my book," I announced.

It wasn't really an untruth. I was going to finish it– eventually.

She squinted at me through her rimless glasses. I felt my face burn like I'd been out in the wind all day.

"I want that book at least half read by suppertime tomorrow, Young Lady," Gran said.

I had backslid from Miss to Young Lady, in spite of doing the dishes. It wasn't really fair, doing homework on Saturday. But there was no use in complaining. Gran would tell me it was my fault, since I'd had the whole six-week marking period to do the assignment. The report due date now loomed just around the corner at the end of Easter vacation.

"Yes 'um," I muttered.

I trudged up the steps to my room, feeling the weight of the book pull at my elbow socket. I went into my room and banged shut the door. I set *Silas* down on my bed. My Timex said 12:15. Gran would nap until at least 2:00. She always took a nap after lunch.

I regularly used candlewax on the window frame, so it slid open without a sound. I squirmed over the sill and onto the porch roof. Next I shinnied down the big oak tree that hugged the side of the porch. Using the hemlocks for cover, I slipped out of the yard onto the path that led to the Voodoo Shack.

Chapter Two

It had been a wet spring. The weather couldn't decide between rain or snow and the ground kept trying to thaw, but all that water had no place to go. Black ooze crept over the sides of my sneakers as I squished my way along the path that wound through Hazard Swamp. The swamp had lots of trees that seemed to be sprouting from little dirt islands. The trees were what made it a swamp instead of a marsh. They blocked most of the light, making the swamp dark and gloomy, even on a sunny day. I shivered, partly because it was kind of creepy and also because I hadn't dared to get my coat off the peg by the back door, since Gran's bedroom was right off the kitchen. I was wearing my heavy wool sweater, but the chill seeped through.

The Voodoo Shack, which stood on a high spot on the edge of Hazard Swamp, was the secret meeting place Alice Pruitt was dying to know about. Greenie Skinner–Deputy Skinner is his pa–was the first I'd asked to join after I discovered the Voodoo Shack in the Hazard Woods about a month ago. I had slipped out of the house, because Gran was looking for me to help with some early spring cleaning even though there were still patches of snow on the ground. I had walked a deer trail into Hazard Swamp and saw a little log cabin tucked away in the woods neat as can be. It was padlocked up tight, but I found the key hanging from a nail on a rickety old woodshed next to the cabin, right next to the sign that said KEEP OUT!

Even though Greenie Skinner was a boy, he was my best friend. Come to think of it, most of my friends were boys. The first thing that I liked about him was his name, Greenie. His real name was Lamonte Green Skinner. Either way, his name was nearly as bad as Iris, and at first we thought maybe only kids with bad-sounding names could become members. Later, Greenie and I had to loosen up the requirements, or have a mighty small membership.

The other good thing about Greenie was that his dad was a deputy sheriff for Harley County, Michigan. It never hurts to be on the good side of the law. The sheriff's office was in Harley City, a few miles from Scottsburg. Our farm was about two miles north of Scottsburg, which is where I'd gone to school since Momma and I moved in with Gran and Gramps four years ago. Folks say the town is so small, you can string a clothesline between the town-limit signs. Harley City was where Momma worked at the hospital as a floor nurse and where we went when we needed to do serious shopping, such as for school clothes or a new toaster.

Anyway, pretty soon Greenie and I let in Cecilia Campbell, because she bribed us with chocolate cup-cakes. Tobey "the Tobster" Koklemeyer got straight A's on his report card and was president of the student council. We figured he was a smart investment. Randy Whip was allowed into the club because he told a good ghost story. He was telling an especially good tale one day about voodoo spells, one thing led to another, and we came up with the Voodoo Shack as a name for the clubhouse. Randy did a great Elvis impersonation, too, though I wasn't sure what all the fuss was about with Elvis Presley. The five of us could sit comfortably around the rickety old table in the Voodoo Shack, so we decided to close the membership.

According to Randy, the cabin was built by Ol' Man Hazard for hunting. It was made up of logs that he had probably cut out of his woods and slapped together with the help of a few beers. Before he died, you never saw Ol' Man Hazard without a Blue Ribbon beer bottle in his hand, except maybe when Deputy Skinner was around. The logs didn't fit too good and left gaps for the wind and varmints to come through. Rags had been stuffed into the cracks, but the mice used those to make nests in the nooks and crannies. The roof was mostly made up of tin sheets that probably blew off somebody's barn. During a strong wind, the roof hummed and rattled so's to give you the creeps.

A rusty set of bunk beds with no mattresses sat along one wall and a table and chairs along another. An old, black wood–burning stove squatted in the corner. The glass of the cabin's only window was cracked and had been mended with duct tape. It was so grimy, not much light came through. Most meetings, we had to use

Greenie's Coleman lantern. A deer head hung crooked on one of the walls. Its mouth was sewed shut into an eerie kind of grin, and its glassy eyes followed you around the room. Its antlers made a good coat rack.

My shoes sloshed with each step as I hurried down the path through Hazard Swamp. I could see that the padlock was already open. Greenie, Randy, and Tobey were already inside sitting around the table. Greenie's Coleman lantern hissed and made weird shadows across their faces.

"Hey, Iris, you're late," Greenie said.

"Where's Cecilia?" I said. The cabin felt cold and damp.

"Doing her book report on *Silas Marner*," Tobey said.

I felt my face heat up a little at the mention of the book.

"Yeah, I'm supposed to be reading it right now. I figure I can whip through it after church tomorrow," I said.

"Darned if I can understand a word of that mumbo jumbo," said Randy. "I'm barely halfway through because I have to keep going back and rereading parts."

"I remember that book from when I was in sixth grade," Greenie said. "I think I got a D minus on my book report. Course, I never read the book."

I could feel the lunch spaghetti churning in my stomach at the mention of a D minus. I pulled my wool sweater around me, but still felt a chill. Under no circumstances was I allowed to get anything less than a C. B's were preferred, and A's usually got me a trip to the Tastee Treat for an ice-cream soda. I had never gotten a D on my report card, but suspected it would earn me summer school, sure as shootin'.

"Well, I guess we better call the meeting to order so's I can get back. Maybe I should read a couple of chapters before bed tonight," I said. "Besides, I'm freezing."

"I, of course, have completed my report," the Tobster said. He smiled at me, showing the gap between his two front teeth. "I would be glad to tutor you, Iris."

My ears felt like they had been caught between two steam irons and I was glad my tangled hair covered them. It was common knowledge that the Tobster had a crush on me. He was one of the few kids in sixth grade who had pimples, but I wasn't about to close any doors at this point. I didn't know what *tutor* meant, but would have rather swallowed gristle than admit it. I guessed I would be pawing through the old dictionary when I got back home.

"Thanks," I said to the Tobster, though I wasn't sure what I was thanking him for. I hoped it wasn't something sinful he was offering to do.

We called the meeting to order. Greenie tore open a package of Fig Newtons he had managed to pinch from home.

"I have obtained some interesting information from the Harley Community Library," the Tobster said, pulling some sheets of paper out of his pocket. "I have taken the liberty of researching this ongoing dilemma about William Hazard's . . . passing. It seems the police are out of leads. Not surprising." The Tobster took a moment to sneer at Greenie, who threw a dirty look back. "Well, guys, read these and tell me what you make of them." He unfolded the papers. They looked like print from a newspaper, but were on regular white paper.

"What the heck are these?" I asked, squinting at the tiny, blurred print.

"They are photocopies of newspaper articles, Iris. They save all the old newspapers for a year, then put them on microfilm," the Tobster said.

I thought about all the old newspapers that continually stacked up in our garage and eventually forced Gramps to park his car in the driveway.

"What's microfilm?" I asked.

"They take a photograph of the documents, then reduce it–something like that. Then you can put it in a machine that enlarges it, so that you can read it. These newspapers, however, hadn't been microfilmed yet."

It didn't make a whole lot of sense to me. First you make something small, then turn around and make it big again. Sounded like a lot of work.

We all crowded around the articles, trying to read them in the bad light. After a lot of shoving, we decided one of us should read them aloud. Naturally, if we wanted to hear what was so all-fired fascinating, we had to let the Tobster do the reading. He cleared his throat, like he was getting ready for some big, important speech.

"This is from the *Harley Gazette,* September 7, 1961," he announced.

"Well, what other newspaper would it be?" Greenie said. The Tobster waved him off and began reading:

"Hubert Angelthorne, owner of FunTyme Amusement, reported that an estimated \$2,000 in cash was missing from the receipts taken in by the amusement company from rides and midway games provided for the Harley County Fair. An audit is being conducted to determine the exact amount of the loss."

"Oh, yeah, I remember when that happened," I said. "All kinds of finger-pointing. Some said the owner was trying to collect insurance."

"Let me continue, please," said the Tobster.

"Local residents hired as temporary workers, as well as regular employees of the company, are being questioned by authorities. Scottsburg resident William D. Hazard was arrested for drunkenness when he allegedly became combative during routine questioning, according to Deputy Walter P. Skinner of the Harley County Sheriff's Department."

I shrugged my shoulders. "So, everybody knows that Ol' Man Hazard liked to drink and fight."

The Tobster gave me a look, so I hushed.

"Hazard had been hired by FunTyme Amusement to operate the merry-go-round. Complaints had been made to management after the merry-go-round was abandoned by its operator for over an hour."

"Ol' Man Hazard was never known for his reliability," Randy said. "He worked for my father for a while. Got canned."

Tobey sighed, like we were all hopeless or something.

"Hey, I remember something," Greenie said. "Yeah, my pa said something about Ol' Man Hazard being away from his post about the time they think the money was stole. Couldn't prove nothin', though."

"Anything–couldn't prove anything," corrected the Tobster with another sigh. "That is what I've been *trying* to tell everybody. But you keep butting in."

"Is there any more?" I asked, yawning. Listening to the Tobster read some newspaper article from the library was an awful lot like doing homework. If I was going to be doing homework, I'd be reading *Silas Marner.*

"Well, that's just about it for this one, except, of course, the mention of a reward."

Now, that woke me up. "Reward?"

"Yep. Of course, this was months ago. I don't know about the reward anymore. But I do know that the money is still missing and the case is unsolved." The Tobster gave Greenie another smirky look.

"Well, Tob, we're all just tickled with your report," said Randy with a tone of sarcasm. He pulled a deck of cards out of his pocket and began to shuffle them. "Poker, anyone?"

I dug into my sweater pocket for my matchsticks. Luckily, I kept a supply in all of my pockets, in case I had to leave the house quiet-like, such as that day. We used kitchen matches to bet with. Every time I burned the trash at home, I would pocket a few extra matches. "Land sakes," Gran would say. "How many matches does it take to burn the trash, Iris? I just bought a box, now it's nearly gone." Since Gran couldn't imagine the *illicit* use I was taking them for, she didn't dwell on the subject.

"Now, hold on, guys, I'm not finished. I've got another whole article here." We tried to ignore him, but he went on reading, trying to carry his voice over the shuffling noise of the cards.

"You gonna ante up, Tob?" Randy asked.

The Tobster held up his hand again, like that was going to get our attention. "This one's from the November 18, 1961, paper," he said.

"Five-card stud, deuces wild," Randy said through a mouthful of Fig Newtons.

I had to give Tobey credit. He kept on reading, even though we had our mind on our game.

"The body of William D. Hazard was found in his hunting cabin, located outside of Scottsburg in Harley County. Sheriff's deputies report that the cause of death is under investigation. It appears that the victim may have been cleaning his gun in preparation for the upcoming firearms deer-hunting season. . . ."

"I'll raise you," I snapped at Greenie, who was wearing his bluffing face. "Heck, Tob, we all know about Ol' Man Hazard blowing his brains out."

The wind had picked up and howled through the tin roof of the cabin.

"Sounds like Ol' Man Hazard's ghost is trying to get in and warm up," said Randy. He looked over the top of his cards at us for a reaction, then added, "Personally, I believe otherwise. He was sitting right where you are, Iris, when somebody did him in."

I could feel the hair on my arms stand up like a bristle brush.

"It is my opinion that he committed suicide," said the Tobster. He had set down his newspaper articles and picked up a cookie. He inspected the cookie, then popped it into his mouth.

"I'll call," I said, shoving in some matchsticks. "Whatcha got, Greenie?"

"Three eights."

"Beats me." I chucked my cards on the table.

Greenie picked up the cards and began shuffling. "Naw, it wasn't suicide, it was an accident."

"My turn to deal," I said, holding out my hand. You had to watch Greenie.

"It wasn't suicide or an accident. That's what they always say when they don't have any clues," Randy said. "My vote's for bloody murder. Maybe somebody wanted that two grand. Maybe it was that guy from the amusement park. Maybe it was hid here in the cabin, and what's his name—"

"Angelthorne," said the Tobster.

"Yeah, and he came looking. Maybe they fought over the gun."

"Well, I think it was Ol' Lady Hazard," I offered. The woman had always given me the willies.

"I don't remember my pa saying anything about Ol' Lady Hazard being a suspect . . . even if it was murder, which I doubt," Greenie said.

"Yeah, well, she gives me the creeps. Five-card draw, one-eyed jacks are wild," I said, dealing the cards. "Cripes, she dresses so weird, and rides that bicycle everywhere like that mean ol' hag in *The Wizard of Oz*." I picked up my cards and was pleased to see a one-eyed jack staring at me, along with a couple of aces. This pot of matchsticks was going to be mine! "Come on, Randy, you gonna bet?"

"Aw, heck, Iris. I can't concentrate with all this talk of murder."

"Not to mention the reward," Greenie said, laying his cards down. "I wonder how much it is. I got my eye on a motorbike."

"Come on, you guys, bet!" I whined. I was holding a gold mine.

"You got five aces or something, Iris?" Randy said.

"Fold," the Tobster said.

"Yeah, me too. I don't have squat," Greenie said.

"I'm out," Randy said. "So, do you think the reward is still good?"

"Dang it, guys, no fair!" I shouted, flinging my cards on the table. I grabbed a cookie and jammed it in my mouth.

"Well, since the money was never found, I would think the reward would still be in place," the Tobster said. "Oh, for heaven's sake, Iris, stop pouting. Here, take my matchsticks."

"Not the same," I mumbled. But I did take the matchsticks.

"Well, if the reward was even ten percent, that would be two hundred dollars. Divided by five, if you count Cecilia, that would be . . ." The Tobster paused, his lips moving silently. "Forty dollars each."

Suddenly, I didn't care about matchsticks anymore.

"Do you think she has the money—Ol' Lady Hazard?" I said.

"Nope," Randy said. "I don't. I think she's looking for it, though."

"Why would she have kilt him, before she knew where the dough was hid?" Greenie said.

"A kilt is a Scottish garment, Skinner," the Tobster said.

"Get off my back, Toadbreath!" Greenie said.

"Quiet!" I yelled. "Maybe it was an accident, killing him. Maybe the gun had a hair trigger or something. Maybe she was trying to scare it out of him, and the gun accidentally went off!"

"And maybe Ol' Man Hazard had a snootful and it went off in his hands, like my pa says," Greenie said.

Randy picked up the cards. I watched my prize hand disappear.

"Well, I think what we got here is a good old-fashioned witch," Randy said.

"Ol' Lady Hazard?" I said.

"Yep. And she's a devious one. Got him to take a special potion, maybe some kind of truth serum with locoweed, bats' ears and frogs' lips and stuff. She mixed it up so's he would tell her where he'd hid the money. But something went wrong, and he blew his brains all over that wall," said Randy, nodding his head toward the wall next to me. "And that's how the window got broken, too, from the shotgun blast," he added.

We all turned our heads and inspected the shadowy wall and cracked window glass. Greenie held the hissing lantern over our heads, but it was still a mite dark.

"I don't see no blood. All's I see is a bunch of cobwebs stuck between these logs," Greenie said.

"Any blood. 'No blood' is bad grammar," the Tobster said. "Blood turns black, you know," he said, squinting in the dim light at the wall. "It would be hard to detect after all these months."

"I suppose they would have cleaned up the brains, so's they could stuff them back in for the funeral," Randy said.

I wished about then that I hadn't had so many Fig Newtons.

"Anyhow, something went terrible wrong. Her little plan backfired," Randy said. "Now he's dead as a doornail, and the money's still . . . somewhere. Maybe right here in this cabin."

"'Cept we've pretty much looked through everything in this cabin and never found so much as a nickel," Greenie said.

"Greenie's right. Only thing we found were a bunch of mouse droppings and those beer bottles over in the corner," I said.

"Well, I'm telling you, it was Ol' Lady Hazard that killed 'im, and if she finds us here, she'll most likely do the same to us," Randy said.

"Yeah, sure, Randy, maybe she'll sneak some toad boogers into our milk at school," Greenie said.

We all laughed, except Randy. His face got beet red.

"My father always says that most answers to life's mysteries can be found at the public library," the Tobster said.

"That's because your pa is a teacher," Greenie said.

"A professor," the Tobster corrected.

"Well, I sure could use that reward money," I said. I thought about my bicycle.

Momma had bought it used from a junky-looking place called Ed's Found Treasures. Gramps had painted it purple–which was my favorite color–and oiled it up. It was getting to be a little small, and the purple was beginning to wear on me.

The Tobster stood and brushed off the seat of his pants. "I would suggest that for our next meeting, we pursue the recovery of this purloined money. Meanwhile, Greenie, see if your father knows if the reward's still being offered. I will be searching for clues in the library."

The rest of us stood to leave. He could be thinking of clues; I would be thinking about my new bike that I would buy with the reward money. It would be a Schwinn three-speed, blue, with silver fenders, and a book carrier on the back. Or maybe wire baskets. And a bulb horn.

Greenie and I always walked together part of the way home, until we got to the split in the path where he headed to town and I went off toward the farm. Some dark clouds were building. We came out of the trees and slogged through black muck and brown marsh grass that was still flattened from the winter snow. The wet was starting to creep up the cuffs of my corduroy pants.

"What would you think if you found out your parents weren't ever married?" I asked Greenie kind of out of the blue.

"Huh?" he said.

"You deaf?" I said in a snippy voice. "What if your folks weren't ever married, I mean before your mother, um, passed on. What would you do?"

"Gee, I dunno. Why?" he asked, and kind of looked at me out of the corner of his eye.

"I just wondered. Can't I ask a question without having a million questions asked back?"

"Well, I–" he started to say, then shrugged his shoulders.

We didn't talk for a while and I pulled up an old cattail and began plucking off the fuzz.

"Alice Pruitt say something to you?" Greenie said.

That near knocked me over. How did he know about her?

"Alice Pruitt is saying things about you, but I don't pay her no mind. Everyone knows she and her ma are gossips. They say things about my pa, too. They're all lies," Greenie said.

"What'd she say about your pa?"

"That he drinks on the job. That since my ma died, he has women riding around in the police car with him at night. Stuff like that."

"Oh" was all I could think to say.

"If she weren't a girl, I'd wallop her a good one."

We didn't talk any more until we got to the split in the path. I felt the first drops of rain.

"Shoot, my shoes are a mess, now I'm gonna get soaked. Gran'll have my hide."

For some reason, neither of us hurried off, in spite of the cold drops that splatted on our heads and ran down our necks. I hunkered farther down into my sweater. The wool always smelled funny when it got wet.

Greenie reached out and kind of touched me on the arm, then pulled his hand back.

He smiled with his mouth, but his eyes looked sad.

"Course, you're a girl and nothing says you couldn't give her what for," said Greenie, smacking his fist into his hand.

"'Cept if Gran found out I was catfighting, I would be grounded until high school."

"Yeah, and Alice the Malice ain't worth it," Greenie said.

The rain had grown steady. I couldn't wriggle my toes anymore, yet Greenie and I stood there like a couple of dopes, looking down at the dead grass and mud around our feet.

"Sit with you at lunch Monday?" I asked.

"Yep. I'll swing by your classroom to get you."

"Okay. See you then."

"Yep."

I ran the rest of the way home. The rain was so cold it took my breath away. I shinnied up the oak tree onto the porch roof and shuffled my way across the slippery shingles to my bedroom window. I about swallowed my tongue when I found it shut and locked up tight as a bank on Sunday.

Chapter Three

Gran had woke up because of the rain. I guess she was bringing me some cookies and milk to help me through my book-reading ordeal, and as she said, was rewarded for her thoughtful deed by finding my room as empty as a church on Saturday night. The rain had been coming in my window, which I had left open from my escape, and naturally she shut *and* locked it. This left me no choice but to go through the kitchen door and find her and Momma sitting at the kitchen table discussing my fate. Momma was in her fresh, crisp nurse's uniform, and I didn't care for the stern look on her face. I hadn't dared to look at Gran at all.

When it was all said and done, it looked like I wouldn't have much to live for for the next couple of weeks. First off, I was given so much work around the house and farm that I might as well have been a prisoner dragging one of those ball-and-chains from my ankle. That wasn't near as bad as the second part of my punishment. I couldn't leave the farm except to go to church and school. The second week of my sentence included Easter vacation, and I felt a big knot in my chest when I figured that out.

After my death sentence was passed down, I stormed out of the house and slammed the door as hard as I dared. I stomped into the barn, where Gramps was trying to fix the Ford tractor. He was doing some cussin' himself. I slammed the door to the barn and I heard a clatter of metal.

"Now durn it, I dropped my wrench," said Gramps. "What in blazes is all the fuss about?"

About then Gramps's mule, Sweetums, let loose with that god-awful racket mules make, half neigh and half bray. I generally brought Sweetums an apple or carrot once or twice a day and he was letting me know what was expected.

"I didn't bring you anything, Sweetums, so hush," I said.

Gramps straightened up from the tractor engine and peered at me through his glasses, which had slipped down his nose. His Ford Motor cap had slid back on his head, and one of the straps of his raggedy coveralls was broke clean off, letting his pants droop. Sometimes Gramps was an embarrassment, but he was my only hope for getting my sentence loosened up.

"Looks like you got in Dutch with Gran, what it looks like to me," he said.

"And Momma," I said, mustering up a look of despair.

"Them women are worse than drill sergeants in the Marines," he said as he climbed on the tractor and pushed the starter. The tractor whined and coughed.

"Weston women are tough ones to reckon with, sure are," Gramps said. "You're showin' signs, too, Iris, of them female family traits."

"Female family traits?" I said.

"Yup. Tough, for one thing. And stubborn as this dang tractor," he said, giving the steering wheel a whack. "And the one that keeps getting you in trouble: doing things your own way, regardless."

"Regardless?"

"Regardless of the consequences. Like the pickle you've got yourself in now. Don't let them two other Weston women fool you, neither. They may be acting all prim and proper when they come down on you, honey, but both your momma and Gran were in more than a speck of hot water in their younger days. Heck, it was your gran's spunk that got me to sparkin' after her in the first place." Gramps let out a little chuckle.

"Well, if I'm so much like them, why do they punish me for it?" I said.

"That's the hun'ert–dollar question. Guess they want to save you from all the trouble you're apt to find by marching in their footsteps. I expect you'll find your own way soon enough, though." Gramps pushed the starter again and the tractor cranked a little stronger.

"Come on, baby, start," Gramps coaxed. The tractor blew a belch of black smoke out its stack and putted to life.

"There she goes! Only thing better'n a Ford is that mule over there," he shouted, looking pleased with himself.

Sweetums hee–haw neighed like he understood the praise. I went over and patted the old mule and gave him a scratch in his favorite spot between the ears. He nosed me for a while, smelling for a treat.

Sweetums was the living half of Gramps's mule team. The half that passed away to mule heaven was Snookums. Gramps tells me he took blue ribbons in the county fair with Sweetums and Snookums. When he gets the chance, Gramps tells the same stories about those mules over and over. Gran tells him to hush, that he's putting everyone into a coma. He back talks her, saying something about cutting her pie crust with a hacksaw. Gramps is the only person I know who dares sass Gran, especially about her cooking.

"Yeah, I guess a mule's okay for pulling a plow," I shouted, half drowned out by the tractor, "but I'm hoping for something fancy someday, like a palomino or pinto horse."

"Well, you can keep on hopin', girlie," Gramps said, raising his voice above the engine noise. "What you want with a horse? Mule's a hun'ert times better. Take you places no horse could go, and lasts a lot longer. By golly, a mule is built by the good Lord to last!"

Truth was, I was attached to old Sweetums but would have rather spent a day in starched underwear than be seen riding him.

"What'd you do this time, Iris?" Gramps said.

"Nothin' at all, except maybe go for a little walk."

Gramps said something back, but the tractor revved up and I couldn't hear him. I pointed to my ear and shook my head.

Gramps shut off the tractor. He pushed his glasses up his nose and gave me a good look. "Last I knew, walking was not illegal, 'less of course it was instead of doin' something like . . . oh, let me see, maybe some chores?"

I jammed my hands deep into my pockets and scuffed my feet in the straw. "Nope. My chores were all done. I took out the trash and burned it, made my bed. Even did my lunch dishes."

"Hmm. I see. What was it that your gran found so offensive about this . . . walk you took?"

"Well, I was supposed to be doing some reading."

"Um–hum. Like maybe some reading of a school-book?"

I nodded.

"So, why'd Gran let you slip right out of the house for this walk, when you were supposed to be reading?"

"Well, I don't suppose she knew."

"Nobody goes in or out of the house without that woman knowin', even if she's sound asleep."

"Well, I kind of left a different way."

Gramps nodded and rubbed his chin like he was checking his whiskers. "Porch roof down the old oak tree?"

My jaw dropped and I just stared at him. "How'd you know?"

"That was my room when I was a boy, you know. Oak tree was still small and I had to use the drainpipe part of the way. Course, I never got caught," he added in a superior tone.

"Well, I never got caught 'til now, and I wouldn't

have if it hadn't started raining. That rousted Gran from her nap earlier than usual."

"Well, I guess you got no choice but to take your medicine," Gramps said. He yanked his glasses off and began rubbing the lenses with an oily handkerchief.

"But isn't the punishment supposed to match the crime? I learned that in school. Shucks, Gramps, they got me doing all the housework *and* I'm grounded for two weeks. Can't even watch *Bonanza*. Can't go see my friends or have anybody over . . . and it's Easter vacation a week from Friday. Us kids got plans."

"So, let me see if I got this straight. You have to do *all* the housework, like all the dusting and sweeping. Probably have you doing the cookin', too."

"Well, no, but if they'd thought of it I probably would."

"Got you scrubbing the kitchen floor and scouring the terlet?"

"Well, not exactly."

"Then what do them two slave drivers expect of you?"

"Well, I gotta do dishes every night, and clean the garage, *and* defrost the fridge. Oh, and they're making me go through my room and box up stuff for the church bazaar."

Gramps whistled softly and shook his head. "That does sound awful harsh."

"*And* besides, I'm grounded. I'd do the work without a peep, I really would, and no TV. But I just gotta be able to leave . . . at least on Thursdays and Saturdays, or my life will be ruined!"

This time he clucked his tongue. "I'm afraid the child protection people will come by and have us all arrested for abuse."

"Now you're making fun," I wailed, and pushed out a couple of tears.

"Now, Iris, I'm not making fun. I know it's serious to you, but we all gotta pay our debts when we're caught."

"But they act like I ran away from home or something. It wasn't but a small thing."

"So, let me get this straight. You admit you did wrong."

"Yes, sir."

"But what you're saying is that they came down too hard on you for what you did?"

I nodded, a few more tears trickled down my cheeks.

"Well, maybe we can appeal the decision . . . plead a lighter punishment."

"One to fit the crime," I said, feeling a glimmer of hope.

"What you got to do, honey, is quit complainin' and get to that schoolbook. Show your momma and gran that you mean to mend your ways. Then maybe after the first week you can go before their ladyships and beg for mercy."

It wasn't exactly the solution I had hoped for, but short of running away and joining a circus, it seemed my only option.

I returned to the house and slammed the door pretty good.

"You want to make it three weeks, Young Lady?" Gran's voice seemed to come from the heavens and it gave me a start. Truth of the matter, she was in the basement, probably doing laundry, and her voice carried up the heat register.

"No, ma'am," I shouted to the register. "I'm going to do my homework now."

"You'll stay in your room if you know what's good for you," warned the register.

I raced up to my room and threw myself on the bed with such a force that *Silas Marner* popped a few inches into the air. There wasn't much to do but open the book. I flipped through it and my eyes caught on a page.

> He had inherited from his mother some acquaintance with medicinal herbs and their preparation–a little store of wisdom which she had imparted to him as a solemn bequest–but of late years he had had doubts about the lawfulness of applying this knowledge, believing that herbs could have efficacy without prayer, and that prayer might suffice without herbs; so that the inherited delight to wander through the fields in search of foxglove and dandelion and coltsfoot began to wear to him the character of a temptation.

It took a while for me to read the page. I had to stop to look up some of the words, but it sure as rain was talking about some kind of medicine that used herbs instead of pills and such. I got to thinking about Ol' Lady Hazard. Was Randy right about her, that she whipped up some potion to make her husband tell her where he'd hid the money?

I reread a sentence in *Silas Marner*, trying to make sense of it all: *began to wear to him the character of a temptation.* It sounded to me like this mixing up of herbal medicine was thought to be closer to the work of the devil than the Lord. I remembered when Gran had smeared a nasty mustard plaster all over me when I had a cold. It smelled so bad that I begged to go back to school before I was better.

It was the word *temptation* that was confusing me. I knew my momma's chocolate cake was a temptation. We all ate that like it was a good thing. Then again, I heard that there were *bad* temptations: sins, like lust and greed and pride, that Reverend Buckman pounded on in his sermons.

I hated to admit to myself that *Silas Marner* was tempting me, but I opened it up, flipped past the introduction to chapter one, *The Weaver of Raveloe*, and began reading.

Chapter Four

———•———

"Land sakes, child, you're dripping a lake all over my clean floor," Gran said.

"Can't help it!"

We'd had no school the Thursday before Good Friday, and Gran decided that was a good time to tackle the freezer. I was trying to carry a big sheet of ice out the kitchen door. The sink was full of stuff we had taken out of the freezer so we could defrost it. We had wrapped the meats in newspapers to keep them. There were dabs of things that had been frozen but not labeled, most of them a mystery. Though Gran said it was a sin to waste food, she allowed that, when we couldn't tell what it was, it was best to pitch it.

Gran had decided to take the chore one step further and clean out the refrigerator section too. The kitchen counter was covered with half bottles of de-fizzed Coke and pickle jars with only the juice left. Somehow, we had three open jars of mustard. I found the chocolate pudding I thought Gramps had finished off, now all thick-skinned and cracked. By the time the sorting was done, I had made two trips to the garbage, and there was a shelf in the fridge completely empty and ready for the Easter ham.

I watched the ice chunks from the defrosting project melt into a puddle in the backyard. Seemed a shame to waste good ice, but I couldn't think of anything useful. I didn't expect Gran would like the idea of me storing it back in the freezer that she'd just chipped it out of.

"Iris, I got another big piece off. We're on the home stretch now, honey," hollered Gran through the screen door.

Gran had been in a lively mood. She always was when she got into a cleaning project. I tried to keep my complaining down, because I was working myself up to asking for parole. I took the chunk of ice out the back door and tossed it in the grass with the rest. I wiped my numb hands on the seat of my pants.

I had gone through my punishment list to make sure everything was checked off. The defrosting project was almost done. I had boxed up old stuff from my room for the church bazaar. Gramps and I had cleaned the garage that Saturday we had our crime-and-punishment talk. He was tickled that we'd made a spot in the garage for his Ford Falcon. The garage had been filled up mostly with a couple years' worth of old newspapers and magazines that we'd saved for the next scout paper drive. We'd heard that the scouts were selling candy bars, instead, to raise money, so we loaded up the papers and hauled them off to the dump, along with soggy cardboard boxes, some rotten boards, my old blow-up swimming pool, and a three-legged table.

I'd gotten through *Silas Marner* in five days. I considered that as near to a miracle as I'd ever know. I'd read it at breakfast, during study time at school, at night before I went to bed, and even in the bathtub. Parts of *Silas Marner* read foreign to me, like Momma's nursing books. But after a while I'd gotten used to it and, bit by bit, it began to read along pretty good. I was more wondering what was going to happen next than worrying about the hardship of reading it.

All the time while I was paying my debt to society, I planned my escape—like a criminal plotting a jail break. Smart way, I figured, was one spoonful of dirt at a time. I'd seen that on a TV show. A convict had dug himself out of his cell with a soup spoon. So, while I was working off my punishment, I was thinking up a way to get to the Voodoo Shack for the meeting that Thursday afternoon.

Gran always said that Tobey Koklemeyer was a good influence on me, unlike "That Skinner Boy." She always called Greenie "That Skinner Boy," and wrinkled her nose a mite. So after everything was loaded back and the fridge was turned on and humming, I took a stab with my imaginary spoon.

"Gran?"

"Mmmm?" she said as she took a final swipe with a rag at the gleaming refrigerator door.

"I was thinking the Tobs—er, Tobey Koklemeyer could help me with my book report."

"Well, then get on the phone and ask that boy over here. Lord knows you could use some of his influence on your schoolwork."

"Um, I was wondering, maybe I could go to his house and work there. That way he wouldn't have to come all the way out here, and it wouldn't be such a big favor and all." I knew that the Tobster would crawl through hot sand for me, but that was beside the point.

"Well, I suppose you could ride your bicycle into town. Make sure he asks his mother." Gran was standing back, smiling at the refrigerator. The smile changed to a frown. "Lordy. I forgot all about the top. Bet there's an inch of dust up there."

She had her head stuck in the broom closet looking for a clean rag when I tiptoed out of the room.

That's how I found myself sitting at the Tobster's dining room table with my copy of *Silas Marner* and my half-finished report in front of me. Tobey had offered to help me finish my report, and taking him up on the offer was the only way I could think of to escape the trials and tribulations of prison life.

The Tobster slid his chair close to mine and was pretending to look over my shoulder like he was reading the report. He breathed through his mouth and I could smell antiseptic mouthwash.

Tobey's mother came in carrying a plate of cookies. She was wearing a red-and-white checked dress and frilly white apron. Her hair was all teased and sprayed, and she must have fallen into a tub of perfume.

"Here we are, children, some nice chocolate-chip cookies. Iris, how are your grandparents and your mother?"

"Just fine, thank you," I said. When I turned to answer Mrs. Koklemeyer, my face bumped the Tobster's hair and I felt a slick of Brylcreem come off onto my forehead. I rubbed at it with my sleeve.

"I know your mother is so busy working at the hospital. What a shame she can never make it to the PTA meetings. It's a blessing she has your grandmother. Whatever would you do without her?" She smiled, like the sewn-in smile of the deer head in the Voodoo Shack.

"Yes 'um," I said.

The Tobster pressed his shoulder into mine as he reached for a cookie.

"Help yourself to some milk or hot cocoa to go with those cookies, but don't spoil your supper. I'm going to get my pot roast in and then go to my hair appointment. Maybe you should invite Alice over. She seems like a bright girl, Tobias."

The Tobster let out a little whimper and squirmed in his chair.

Mrs. Koklemeyer strutted out of the room, but her perfume stayed. We heard her clattering around the kitchen, humming a little tune.

"Tobias?" I said.

"Yeah, so?" he said.

Being burdened with a bad name myself, I decided not to press the matter. It was mention of Alice the Malice that made my neck hair bristle.

"Why does she think you would want to invite *her*?" I whispered.

Tobey shrugged and started to read my report out loud.

"Silas Marner was a poor peasant who wove things for the rich people. He kept having spells, and people wondered if he was possessed. He got accused of stealing from the church and maybe killing a man. It was really his best friend who stole the money . . ."

"I'm leaving now," shouted Mrs. Koklemeyer.

"Bye," Tobey and I yelled together.

We heard the kitchen door shut, and the sound of her car starting and driving off. A smile crept up on me. I was thinking of ways to convince the Tobster that we should head out to the Voodoo Shack, when his sweaty hand slid over mine. I jumped up so fast that my chair knocked over with a clatter.

"Let's go for a walk," I shouted.

The Tobster put my chair right and ran his hand through his oily hair.

"Where do you want to go," he said.

"Oh, maybe Hazard Swamp."

"The swamp! I thought I could buy you a cherry Coke at the Tastee Treat," Tobey said. He jammed his fists in his pockets. "Besides, I got on my good pants."

"So, go change them. I'm going to the Voodoo Shack. I can't miss the meeting. Maybe someone's got an idea where Ol' Man Hazard hid that money he stole. I was thinkin' maybe it was buried in the woodshed."

"Aren't you still grounded? What about your home-work?"

"In answer to your first question: none of your business. In answer to your second . . ." I picked up my book report, folded it, and jammed it in my shirt pocket. "I'll take it with me."

He glanced at his watch and scowled. "The other kids won't be there for a while." Then he smiled. "Or did you want us to be alone?"

"Maybe." I gave him a little smile back.

I wasn't proud of myself, but I didn't want to miss the meeting. I couldn't go without him, it was too risky.

"Well, okay, but give me a minute to change, or I'll get in trouble with Mother."

He took forever. Probably hanging up his good pants so's not to wrinkle them. When he finally came back into the dining room, I noticed that he had added a new layer of Brylcreem foam to his hair and smelled like my Gramps's Old Spice, only ten times stronger. I rushed out the door ahead of him before I choked from the fumes.

"Hey, Iris, wait up. You have to wait, because you don't know the way from my house. You sure you don't want a cherry Coke first?"

"No! Now, come on, slowpoke!" I gasped in the fresh air. "I can find the Voodoo Shack with or without you," I shouted over my shoulder. I looked back and saw the Tobster stumbling down the porch steps after me.

"Oh, yeah? Then why are you going the wrong way?"

He had me there. I changed directions and he caught up. I didn't have to look, I could smell him.

"And keep it down. We're walking right past Alice Pruitt's house," he hissed at me. "Do you want her to follow us?"

I looked up at the Pruitts' big old brick house. I couldn't help but stare at those weird stone lions on the front porch that looked like they belonged in front of a museum. The house looked a little shabby, with the shutters and trim just starting to peel and the back porch sagging.

"You never answered me–back at your house," I said. "Why did your mother think we should invite *her* over?"

"Mother says it would *behoove* me to make friends with Alice," the Tobster said.

"Friends! Why?"

"Well, you see, Mrs. Pruitt is the head of some la-de-da ladies' club, Daughters of the American Revolution, and Mother wants to join. Mother says it wouldn't kill me to be nice to Alice, maybe take her out for a Coke."

"What the heck's the Daughters of the American Revolution?"

"Beats me. I took her for ice cream once–"

"What!"

"Now hold on, Iris. Mother made me. Anyway, all Alice did was go on and on about herself, and how her father had been a brilliant surgeon before he died of a heart attack, and how she's going to beat me in the next student council election–"

"How could you go for ice cream with *her*? She's stuck-up, and rats her hair up so much, and uses tons of hair spray, *and* she wears makeup–which doesn't cover up her pimples, if that's what she thinks. But the worse thing is that she looks down on everybody like we're dirt. Her mother said terrible things about my momma and me, and now Alice is telling everybody."

"Don't you see, Iris? The only way to keep her from being an enemy is to be her friend." The Tobster sighed. "She's an absolute bore." He smiled. "Not like you, Iris. You're a lot of fun."

My ears were starting to burn. I glanced at the Pruitt home. Last thing I needed right now was to see her snotty face in the window. The house was dark.

"Maybe she's not home," I said.

"Maybe," said the Tobster. "But just in case, let's double-back a couple of times."

We came to a little woods, and the Tobster led me down a path that you couldn't see from the road. I kept looking back for Alice, but never saw her. We even stopped a half dozen times when I thought I heard noises, but then everything was quiet. Twice we changed direction, like we were going back to the Tobster's. No Alice.

We came to a small dirt road, like a farm road. "I don't think she followed us," Tobey said.

"Naw, she's probably off doing some stupid thing, like waxing her shoes or something," I said. "Where does this road go?"

"To Mrs. Hazard's house."

"Wow! You ever been there?"

"Heck no! Can't you see the no-trespassing signs all over the place?"

"Yeah, so? Those are just left from last huntin' season, is all. I think we should go down there and spy. Maybe we'll get a clue about that stolen money."

"Are you insane? It's bad enough that we tramp all over the cabin like we own it. No way am I going to sneak up on Mrs. Hazard. That would definitely be against the law."

"You're just chicken," I said.

The Tobster kind of flared his nostrils at me. "Well, I'm not going, and that's final! Are we going to the meeting or not?"

"Yeah, okay," I said, glancing over my shoulder at the dirt road. I just had to see where she lived. I imagined a dilapidated old mansion, shutters hanging, doors creaking, and spiderwebs draped all over everything.

In the basement she would be hunched over a boiling kettle of her latest concoction, a black cat watching as she stirred the brew. "Come in, dearie!" she would cackle, somehow knowing I was watching her, "and have a little of my truth serum!"

"Iris! You coming?"

"What? Oh, sorry, Tob. I was just thinking—"

"Forget it!" The Tobster was babbling on and on, warning me, I guess.

But of course I wasn't listening.

Chapter Five

———•———

"It's just around this bend," Tobey said.

It was a good thing I hadn't tried to find the Voodoo Shack on my own, because I was all turned around every which way by the time we spotted the glint off the tin roof of the cabin.

Then I got the feeling, real strong, that made me stop dead in my tracks.

"What?" Tobey said.

"Shhh, I heard something," I whispered. "Hear that?"

We stood still as rocks and listened. There was a noise, it was kind of a chunking noise. It came real regular: *chunk chunk chunk*. It was coming from the direction of the cabin.

Chunk chunk chunk.

The noise stopped sudden-like and I all but quit breathing, my ears straining.

We inched closer. I watched not to snap any twigs underfoot.

Chunk chunk chunk—clink.

We stopped dead again, listening hard.

"Dang it, another blasted rock!"

"Somebody's there!" whispered the Tobster. "Maybe it's Greenie or Randy."

"Shhh, quiet," I hissed at him.

My knees felt like Silly Putty and I wasn't sure they would hold me. I didn't care if the Tobster's hand was all sweated up, I was gripping it so tight, he let out a little yelp.

"Shhh!"

I let go of his hand and dropped to my hands and knees. The Tobster did the same and we crawled toward the cabin.

There was a rattling noise. We got close enough to get a good view of the Voodoo Shack and the clearing around it. Someone was at the door and it wasn't one of the gang. The first thing I noticed was a bright splotch of green moving through the trees. I could only see the back of a woman wearing a tenty dress that was the color of green apples. Her head was covered with a scarf—red. She had a shovel in her hand. She leaned the shovel against the cabin and looked around. Then I got a glimpse of her face. Next she shuffled back to a wheelbarrow that she must have brought along, and pushed it a ways to the woodshed, where she tipped it up.

"It's Ol' Lady Hazard! What the heck is she up to?" I croaked.

Ol' Lady Hazard shook her fist. "Blast you, Bill Haz-ard," she yelled, and kicked at nothing. Next she turned toward the Tobster and me, and we shrank down real fast into a bramble patch. She kept yelling like she was crazy or something. "Where is it? What have you done with it?" She stomped around like in a full fit and then started coming right toward us. I never felt my heart thump so fast as I did right then. Just when she was close enough to trip right over us, she stopped, then kind of slouched next to a tree, and just stared off into the woods.

She kept up the funny faraway look, like a trance, for what seemed an hour. The Tobster and I didn't dare move, so we just stayed crouched in the brambles with thorns poking us all over. Then Ol' Lady Hazard blinked a couple of times and looked around like nothing at all had happened. She turned and walked back toward the cabin and got her shovel. Just when I was thinking about moving my leg that had gone numb, she looked back right to where we were hiding. I guess she didn't see us because next she turned around and disappeared off into the woods, dragging her shovel along beside her.

We stayed down for a while longer. The only noise was a crow cawing at us and the sound of my heart pounding in my ears. I heard the Tobster grunt and stand up. His face was pasty white and dripping with sweat. He brushed himself off, then reached down to give me a hand, but I got up on my own.

"Well, I guess that clinches it," I said. My voice had a catch.

"Wha–what?" the Tobster said. He was having trouble talking, too.

"She's looking for that money, sure as shootin'."

•   •   •

It was only the Tobster and me who had seen Ol' Lady Hazard doing her strange deeds. By the time Randy, Greenie, and Cecilia had come upon us, Ol' Lady Hazard had stalked off down the path, leaving holes and little piles of dirt everywhere.

We all walked around inspecting the holes.

"I knew it!" Randy said. "Ol' Man Hazard buried that money somewhere out here, and she's lookin' for it."

"Well, she's not plantin' daisies, that's for sure," I said.

Eventually, we got tired of looking at the holes and straggled into the Voodoo Shack to discuss the situation.

"What's everybody talking about?" Cecilia whined. She had brought macaroon cookies—my personal favorite—and we were all stuffing them in our mouths and speculating about what we had just seen.

"That's what you get for missing the last meeting," said Randy. "We had a discussion about Ol' Man Hazard's murder and the lost money that he stole."

"But I thought he had some kind of hunting accident," Cecilia said.

"It *was* a hunting accident," Greenie broke in.

"Like heck it was. Look, did you find out about the reward money?" Randy said.

"What reward?" Cecilia asked. "What's going on, you guys?"

We all ignored her and kept eating the cookies. The pile was going down fast.

"Pa says he thinks it's still good, but was wondering why I wanted to know," Greenie said.

"What'd you tell him?" I asked.

"I changed the subject real quick."

"I spoke with my father, and he indicated that the best approach to any enigma is to make organized notes." That was the Tobster's brilliant contribution.

"What the heck's an ig–" Cecilia and her questions.

"It's a puzzle, a riddle. What we have here, guys, is a mystery wrapped in an enigma," the Tobster spouted.

We had all been talking at once, but stopped dead and stared at Tobey.

"What in blazes are you yappin' about, Toad?" said Greenie.

The Tobster cleared his throat. "The mystery–the demise of Mr. Hazard–is wrapped in an enigma, which is like another puzzle, and that is the missing money."

"Why don't you just call it one big fat mystery?" I snapped. I was getting tired of Mr. High and Mighty's fancy words. Besides, I was still ticked off that he had taken Alice Pruitt out for ice cream.

"Well–I–my father . . ."

"Oh, put a sock in it, Koklemeyer," said Greenie. "I still say it was an accident, but I do know for sure that there is some money missing, and that there is a motorbike in Harley City with my name on it."

"And a Schwinn bicycle for me," I added.

"I'm getting a guitar with my share," Randy said. "I'm gonna do Elvis songs, maybe cut a record . . ."

"I think I'll purchase a new thesaurus," the Tobster said.

"That figures," I mumbled. "What are you gonna get, Cecilia?"

"Huh?"

We all reached for the last macaroon. "Dibs," I shouted, slapping away everybody's hands.

"So, what do we do next?" Randy asked.

"I don't know about you, but I'm going home to finish my book report," Cecelia said. "You guys have me all confused."

"Yeah, I guess I should get going, too," Randy said.

"I think I'll work on my book report here," I said, pulling my somewhat crumpled papers out of my pocket. I smoothed them out some and lay them on the table. I could feel the Tobster looking at me. I didn't look back. I had decided to keep my mouth shut about my plans. It was plain and simple that the next thing to do was to check out Ol' Lady Hazard's place, look for more clues. There was a reason she was digging all those holes, and I was going to get to the bottom of it.

We all went outside to take another look at the holes that Ol' Lady Hazard had dug. Randy and Cecilia got bored after a while and headed for home. I was stalling, waiting to carry out my plans.

"You've got to come back to the house with me, Iris," whined the Tobster, as if reading my mind. "Your bicycle is still there."

I had forgotten all about my bicycle. He stood staring at Greenie and me. Good ol' Tobey. Probably still hoping to get me soused on cherry Cokes at the Tastee Treat.

Just then something white in one of the holes caught my eye. I stooped and reached in the hole to fetch it out. It was just an old piece of paper. I figured Ol' Lady Hazard had dropped her shopping list or something during her digging frenzy. Interesting: a witch's shopping list. The paper was from a spiral notebook, pale green, not white, and lined. It looked well worn and was smudged with dirt.

"Whatcha got there?" Greenie said.

I unfolded the paper and looked at the writing. Greenie and the Tobster leaned in to read along. Most of the Old Spice had worn off the Tobster, and both of the boys smelled a little like Gramps's mule on a hot day.

"Well, what do you make of this?" I said, and began reading the four lines scrawled across the paper.

Go thru the bog and into the logs
And youl find what I have did.
Think like a buck and youl have sum luck
To find where the treasure is hid.

It sure wasn't a shopping list.

"Well, whoever wrote this has atrocious spelling and grammar," the Tobster said. "Did you drop this, Greenie?"

Greenie made a grab for Tobey.

"Knock it off," I said, slapping Greenie's hand down. "Don't you guys see what this is?" I said in a loud whisper.

"Yeah, it's one of them poems," Greenie said.

"Actually, it's more of a riddle . . . another enigma. Let's see, an enigma wrapped in a mystery surrounded by another enigma," the Tobster said.

I was about ready to explode. I wanted to knock them both silly.

"It's a treasure map . . . sort of . . . you dummies," I snapped.

"I don't see no map," Greenie said. He took the paper from me and turned it over to look at the backside.

"Any map," the Tobster said.

Greenie took another lunge at the Tobster. I grabbed for the poem/riddle/enigma/treasure map and heard it tear.

"Now, blast it all, you two, see what you've done," I said, trying to match the two pieces back together.

They stopped horsing around and looked at me. The Tobster's face was beet red and Greenie's lip was turned up in a snarl.

"If you'd settle down for one second, maybe we can break the code on this thing," I said.

"What code?" Greenie said. "Darn it all, Iris, you're seeing a lot of things on that piece of paper that just ain't there."

The Tobster opened his mouth to speak, then thought better of it.

"I bet anything that if we can figure out this code . . ."

"Actually, it's an enigma," interrupted the Tobster.

"Okay, figure out this enema . . ."

"EN–IG–MA," the Tobster corrected.

". . . we can find the stolen money. Jiminy Cricket, you guys," I said, waving the pieces of paper around. "This is our first real break in the case. Don't you see?"

"I dunno," Greenie said.

The Tobster shrugged and jammed his hands into his pockets.

"I'm taking charge of this," I said, carefully folding the torn pieces and putting them in my pocket. "Next meeting, we'll show Randy and Cecilia."

"Well, I gotta go and do my paper route," Greenie said, and then he headed off down the path toward his house.

Tobey glanced at his watch. "We'd better get going."

"I'm gonna stay here for a while and think about this," I said.

"Come on, Iris. You're not still considering going to Mrs. Hazard's house, are you? Well, you can count me out." He was whining again. "I thought maybe we could still have a Coke or something."

"Maybe you should take *Alice*," I said in a snippy voice. It was a mean thing to do, but I had to get rid of him somehow.

It worked. His nostrils flared and he stalked off down the path. He told me I would be sorry. He was right.

I would have sworn that a cold wind came up when I turned down that dirt road to Ol' Lady Hazard's place. The sun went under some clouds. Trees seemed to crowd the road, making it like a dark tunnel. The house wasn't at all like I had expected. It was small and square, with white peeling paint. There were lots of doodads all over the yard: cement elves and toadstools and other statues half buried in long, brown grass. I was crouched at the edge of the woods, spying between the trees across the yard. It was all ragged and brown, like yards look at the end of winter. She had a garden, but it was too early to be planted. Everything seemed kind of sad and neglected. I was dying to see the inside, certain that I would find some answers, if I only had the guts to sneak up and look.

A lot of smoke was coming from the chimney, like she had a roaring fire going, so I figured she had made it back from her hole–digging escapade. I imagined her doing her witch things, chopping up eyes of newt and such. Maybe she was stirring a big ol' pot of something or studying up in her witchcraft books to get some *illicit* power to steer her toward the stolen money.

I crept along the tree line for a better look. Maybe I could get a peek in the window, or even find another clue. I didn't know what it would look like, but I was sure I would know a clue when I saw it.

It about knocked me over, what I did see, and it wasn't a clue. There, sitting pretty as you please, was Gramps's Ford Falcon in the driveway. And it wasn't just a car *like* Gramps's, either. It was the real thing. It had the orange ball on the antenna that he'd put on last winter when the snow was plowed real high. He'd left it on come spring because Gran said it helped her find the car when it was in the big parking lot at the supermarket in Harley.

But it wasn't Gramps who came sashaying out of the squealing door. Nope, it was Gran, plain as day, who marched down the steps, carrying a sack. I thought my jaw was going to drop right off my face when I saw her!

"Now, Blanche," I heard Gran say, "I don't think you charged me enough."

"Nonsense," Ol' Lady Hazard said, waving her hand back and forth like a bee was after her. "It's me who owes you. I can't tell you what a help it is to have someone to share my burdens with. I just had to tell *someone* the truth. I have been holding it inside for so long. . . ."

Ol' Lady Hazard was still wearing her apple green tent dress. Now she had a maroon shawl draped over her shoulders. I'd never seen two colors clash more. She looked like she was fighting back a few tears. I wondered if that truth was how she had done in Ol' Man Hazard, trying to get the *truth* out of him about that carnival money that he had stolen. Now Gran was probably in on that truth—whatever it was. It was another one of Tobey's enigmas. Then Ol' Lady Hazard said something about Gran taking the *tonic* twice a day in something or other. I wondered if Gran knew who, *what*, she was dealing with?

Holy smokes! Now that Gran was an accomplice, would she have to do her in, too? Maybe Gran had fallen under Ol' Lady Hazard's spell. What was she doing getting tonic from her: a crazy old woman who had probably killed her husband.

I watched, my heart thumping and my head spinning, as Gran climbed into the Falcon and started it up. Ol' Lady Hazard stood on the house's rickety porch and waved just as friendly as you please while Gran pulled out. Then, I swear, Ol' Lady Hazard had that spell she had back at the Voodoo Shack. She just kind of stared toward the woods where I was hunkered down. I would have bet my purple bike she was looking right at me but wasn't seeing me. As quick as it started, it was over. She kind of straightened up real tall, then went into the house.

Just then my life flashed before me as I caught a glimpse of my watch. I would never make it home before supper. I still had to get my bike from the Tobster's. I raced down the dirt road, found the path through the woods, and burst from the trees onto the street where Tobey lived. I slowed to a jog; my legs felt like rubber and I was sure someone had planted a knife in my rib cage. Maybe it was a knife in my heart I was feelin', seeing Gran coming from Ol' Lady Hazard's! Was Gran in cahoots, or in danger?

Then my pounding heart near stopped dead because of what I saw. Up ahead, in the Tobster's driveway, sat Momma's station wagon.

Chapter Six

———•———

Momma and I were the only customers at the Tastee Treat Sweet Shoppe and Mercantile. We sat at the soda counter sipping cherry Cokes. It was confusing to me why everybody wanted me to have a cherry Coke, most of all Momma. I couldn't look at her, not right away. My face went all hot, just remembering how I had stood puffing and panting in front of Mrs. Koklemeyer and her.

There hadn't been much use in pretending I had been doing homework. The explanation that the Tobster and I had gone for a little walk got Mrs. Koklemeyer going in her squeaky voice about the Tobster's torn shirt and muddy pants. She had sent him off to take a bath and put iodine on his bramble scratches. Momma thanked Mrs. Koklemeyer and marched me out of the house. She put my bicycle in the back of the station wagon and acted like I wasn't even there. I slid into the front seat and we drove off. Next thing I knew, we were sitting at the Tastee Treat with our cherry Cokes.

Momma sighed and took a swallow of drink. Her hair was pulled into a ponytail. Everything she wore was black: slacks, sweater, and her prized French beret. Gran called it her beatnik beanie. I thought it looked pretty spiffy, myself.

I sucked my glass dry and the straw made a gurgling noise. Gran would have scolded me for sure, but Momma didn't seem to notice.

She sighed again and smoothed back some hairs that had escaped from her ponytail. They stayed put for only a second, then fell back down.

"I thought it would be a nice surprise to pick you up from the Koklemeyer's," Momma said. "Then you wouldn't have to ride your bike all the way home."

"Yes 'um." I didn't know what else to say. I kept waiting, expecting Momma to tell me how she was disappointed in me and maybe to ground me for the whole next summer vacation. Truth was, it was making me a little nervous, her sitting there sighing and staring into her Coke glass.

"I figured I could spend some time with my little girl. I know we don't do enough things together. It's not fair to your gran, having to do for you all the time. She's getting old, you know."

"Uh-huh," I said.

"And your gramps, bless his heart, worried that you don't have a dad, and trying to be one for you."

Gramps was just Gramps and I'd never much thought about him trying to be a dad. I did figure if it weren't for Gramps, I would probably have had bars on my bedroom windows by now. I wondered about my father, what he was like. Sometimes I could feel an empty spot inside me. Maybe that was where my father belonged.

"You've been getting in trouble lately, Iris."

I stared into my empty Coke glass. My mouth was cotton-ball dry, and I wished I hadn't guzzled my soda so fast.

"I s'pose it's to get attention. Well, Lord knows, maybe you could use a little more attention from your mother."

She was interrupted by a skinny kid behind the counter. He adjusted his paper hat and asked if we wanted another soda pop. Momma ordered me another. No matter how much I drank, I couldn't wash down the lump stuck in my throat.

"You know I have to work. Gran and Gramps couldn't support all of us without my paycheck from the hospital."

I nodded. I knew my momma couldn't stay home and bake chocolate-chip cookies and whip up a pot roast like Mrs. Koklemeyer. She was always working or sleeping or tired.

"How do you feel about that, Iris?" Momma slid her hand on mine and gave it a squeeze.

I shrugged, afraid to try and talk.

She continued to hold my hand and we sipped our Cokes.

"Your father and I loved each other very much."

She said that out of the blue, without so much as a hint from me.

I looked at Momma. Her cheeks were wet and she swiped at them with the back of her hand.

I wanted to ask her if she and my father had been married. I knew wives usually took their husbands' names when they married. Momma and I had the same name as Gran and Gramps: Weston. I guessed if she and my father had gotten married, she had never bothered to change her name. More than anything, though, I wanted to know about my father–what he was like. How tall was he? What color was his hair? What jokes did he tell? Had he been handsome or goofy looking? I saw a picture of my father in my head, but it was blurred.

Momma seemed to read my thoughts. "We met in a MASH unit. That stands for Mobile Army Surgical Hospital."

"In the Korean war?" I said.

She nodded. "We were both stationed there. Me, as a nurse, and Roger–your father–was in charge of transportation, like the jeeps and trucks and stuff. He was a corporal, then got promoted to sergeant."

She smiled but not at me. I reckon she was thinking about my dad, Sergeant Roger.

"We celebrated that night, when he was promoted." I saw my momma's cheeks grow red. She took a look at me out of the corner of her eye.

"That was a wonderful night, Iris. You know why?"

"Why, Momma?"

"Because, honey, that was the night you were conceived."

I looked at her, not sure what she meant.

"I got pregnant with you, sweetie. It just happened, so unexpected like."

Now it was my cheeks that burned red hot. I couldn't believe she was using that word *pregnant*. Part of me wanted to slide under the soda counter and part of me wanted to hear more.

Momma ran her hand down my hair and picked out a piece of branch that was stuck in there.

"Such a tomboy, my little girl. Roger would have loved you so much . . . he . . ." Momma started to cry. Just then the stupid guy in the paper hat asked if we wanted anything else. I gave him a dirty look and he slapped down our bill and disappeared through a door into the back.

"Momma?"

"Yes, Iris?"

"What was he like–my father–I mean . . . I . . . did you, were you ever . . ." Now I was the one who turned on the waterworks.

"Iris?"

Momma put her arm around my shoulder like she was trying to stop the shaking. Hard as I tried, I couldn't get the words out to ask Momma if they'd ever gotten married.

"Were we in love? Is that what you wanted to ask?"

I shook my head, and wiped at the wet on the counter with my napkin.

"What, then, honey?"

"When you were in the army, did you ever get . . . were you ever . . ."

The Paper Hat Kid hung around and fiddled with a

spring–loaded paper–napkin dispenser, pushing it in again and again with annoying little clicking noises. Just then there was a tinkle of a bell announcing somebody coming in the door. Much to my horror, I was looking at Alice Pruitt and her mother searching one of the store shelves.

"You could have given me more time to get things for your party, Allison," Mrs. Pruitt said. "Now tell me again who the girls are that you invited," she said real loud like all the world should hear.

Alice looked over at me and smirked. "Well, Mother, *you* told me who to invite. You know, the daughters of those ladies in *your* club."

I guess I was supposed to turn green with envy.

"Yes, my DAR society. Heavens, these paper plates will never do. Young man, do you have anything more suitable for a young lady's party? These are for small children and are rather silly." Mrs. Pruitt lifted her head and looked toward the counter. Paper Hat Kid nearly dropped the napkin dispenser, and little folded napkins shot all over the place.

"Um, no, ma'am. Them's all we've got," he sputtered, scooping up the jumble of napkins.

Then Mrs. Pruitt acted like she had just seen Momma and me, but I knew darn well she had spotted us when they came in.

"Well, hello, Carolyn," Mrs. Pruitt said in a voice like she'd just found a dead skunk in her garage. "Look, Allison, it's . . . Daisy."

"Iris," I mumbled. I hoped that neither of the Pruitts could see that Momma and I had been blubbering. I wanted to blow my nose but was afraid it would give me away.

"Iris. Yes, of course," she said, and kind of sniffed like she smelled a toot. "Such an ... old-fashioned name. Charming. Of course, my Allison is named after her great-great grandmother. She ..."

I kind of tuned her out and I guess Momma did, too, because all of a sudden Mrs. Pruitt's voice got sharp.

"Carolyn, didn't you hear me?" she snapped. "Gracious, I think it's so sad when a woman has to work and is too tired to be civil–"

"Pardon me, Roberta, did you say something?" Momma's voice was cool and smooth.

"I *said,* Do you believe the selection in this town?"

"Well, Roberta," Momma said, "it *is* a small town." I smirked. Momma was talking right back down to Mrs. Pruitt, though it seemed to go right past her.

"And look what they want for this dusty old package of paper plates–a mere dozen!" she complained to no one in particular. "Seventy-nine cents!"

"Mooootherrrr," Alice whined, "they have little bears on them. I wanted Barrrrrbieeee. Can't we go to Harrrleeey?"

"We don't have time, darling, I have to make the scones. Next time, give me more notice." She patted Alice on the shoulder, like it was the end of the world that they had to have their stupid scones–whatever those were–on teddy-bear paper plates. I smirked again, imagining Alice and her hoity-toity friends having their refreshments on paper plates made for kindergartners.

"Can't we use the chiiiiinaaaaa, Moooootherrrr!" Alice's voice was getting real shrill, and I thought I saw Mrs. Pruitt wince.

"Perhaps next time, precious. Young man! Do I have to stand around all day waiting to pay for this over-priced package of paper plates?"

The Paper Hat Kid shuffled over to the cash register and rang up the sale.

Mrs. Pruitt turned to Momma and me and gave a sharp little nod and one of those sniffs again. Alice looked like she was working up to a full-fledged hissy. If I'd acted like that, Gran would have had my hide for sure.

As the Pruitts were leaving, a herd of kids burst into the store and swarmed to the candy counter. Paper Hat stood at attention, waiting to ring up the penny and nickel sales.

"Well, Iris, things are getting a little busy here."

I nodded.

Momma looked like a sail that had lost its wind. She smiled at me, then opened her purse, got out her change purse, and left some money on the counter. She dug around for a handkerchief, then pulled out some napkins, which had been jammed every which way into the holder, and honked into them. We both laughed.

We slipped off our stools and headed for the car.

"Momma?"

"Um–hum?"

"Got one more question."

She stopped and looked at me, but somewhere between the door of the Tastee Treat and the car I'd lost my nerve to ask Momma about ever being married. I had to ask her *something.*

"What are we gonna tell Gran? I mean, about me being, um, gone this afternoon."

Momma started to laugh and opened the door for me to squirm into the car. She was still laughing when she climbed into the driver's seat. She looked at my streaked face, dirty clothes, and tangled hair.

"Now I guess we got a *real* problem, don't we?" she said.

"Yep. And we only got a little ways to home to think up a solution," I said. "And without lying, of course."

"Of course," Momma said, "without lying."

Chapter Seven

———•———

Turned out we didn't have to worry about Gran questioning my afternoon activities because she had taken to bed with a headache. It must have been a doozie of a headache to keep Gran down when it was time to start supper. Momma took Gran's temperature and told her to stay put. I went upstairs for a bath and when I came back down, Momma was frying hamburgers. I clanged the bell to call Gramps in from the barn. I had a twinge of worry when Gran didn't come to the table to eat. Momma heated her some soup, which she barely touched.

Good Friday morning, Gran was in the kitchen making breakfast. The toast was burnt, the eggs like rubber. Bacon grease smoked and nearly caught fire because she forgot to turn off the burner.

Gramps told her to get to bed, that he and I'd take care of things in the kitchen. She would have none of it, though, and shook a wooden spoon at him. When Momma got home after working all night, she found Gran slumped over the kitchen counter, coughing like her whole insides would come out.

Momma and Gramps got Gran to bed, and I was told to go upstairs and start getting ready for church. I didn't go up, though, but hung around the kitchen door, listening.

"Now, Carolyn, I'll be fine after a little nap. Lord knows I've weathered worse spells," Gran said.

"You're runnin' a fever. You've caught a bug," Gramps said.

"I don't have a bug!" Gran raised her voice like she had just been insulted. "I'm . . . just . . . tired."

"Your temp's over a hun'ert. Isn't that right, Carolyn?" Gramps said.

"More like one oh two. Dad's right, Mom. I'm calling the doctor. See if they can squeeze us in this afternoon," Momma said.

"I'm not going to the doctor. Besides, maybe you forgot it's Good Friday. The office will be closed. Now, both of you, I'll be . . ." Gran didn't finish. She started that coughing that made my insides hurt just listening.

"What I need . . . leave me alone . . ." Then she coughed some more and I heard Momma rushing to the kitchen. I stood close against the wall in the dining room so Momma wouldn't see me. I could hear her fill a glass of water and go back into the bedroom.

"I don't get sick, 'cept maybe from worry—Give me that dang glass, Carolyn. Land sakes, I can hold on to it myself."

"You're spillin', Mom. Let me steady it. Don't be so ornery."

"Last time was when you were off gallivanting overseas in Korea. Got sick as a dog, I did. It's the worry does it to me . . ." Her cough sounded more like a gasp this time. "Worried sick about you, over there in the family way. Lord have mercy, I– Get that dang glass of water out of my face, Carolyn . . ." This time the coughing didn't stop until Gran upchucked.

"Never mind now, Mom. Just lean over the side. Don't worry about the mess," Momma said.

I wiped the wet off my cheeks, but more came. It stung the corners of my eyes and trickled to my mouth. I licked it away. It tasted salty and warm.

"There's just one thing that'll put me right as rain– and it isn't any doctor or drugstore medicine. Worked before . . ." Gran's voice trailed off.

"Hush and lie down."

I tiptoed upstairs to get ready for church, though I had a feeling we wouldn't be going.

Was Gran's worrying about me making her sick? I didn't mean to be so troublesome all the time. I guessed I didn't think things out like I should.

I took off my clothes, folded them, and put them on the floor in my closet. I could wear them again, they weren't too bad. I slipped into my robe and went down the hall to the bathroom. I watched the tub fill, tested the water, and stepped in. It was a little hot, but it felt right– to near scald myself. Soaping a washcloth, I thought about Gran taking sick so quick. If it wasn't her worrying about me, then maybe it was something else made her sick. Maybe she just plain picked up a bug somewhere. Gran was right, though, she *never* got sick. And it seemed so sudden. She had been fine, that morning, before–

I bolted up, sloshing water everywhere. *Before* she

went to Ol' Lady Hazard's. That was it! Just what kind of tonic did Ol' Lady Hazard give Gran? And what was the "burden" that Ol' Lady Hazard had shared with Gran? Now that she had passed along some deep, dark secret, did she need to do away with Gran? Why did she tell her to begin with?

I scootched down into the water and watched the steam rise. It went up for a while, then vanished, like magic. More followed, going up, up, then it would disappear. It reminded me of the mist rising off the pond in Hazard Swamp. Sometimes it gave me the creeps—everything wrapped up in that thick haze, all twisted and weird. I closed my eyes and felt myself rise with the mist, floating and drifting.

Why would Ol' Lady Hazard try to do Gran in? Was she a witch? Then she wouldn't need a reason. Maybe Ol' Lady Hazard gave her a deadly tonic. Maybe it was an experiment. Maybe she knew it was a mistake to share her secret with Gran, and now she had to do her in. I remembered that I still had the riddle/treasure map/enigma thing. I had taped it back together and tucked it into my copy of *Silas Marner.* I wondered how bad Ol' Lady Hazard would want it back.

I was getting cold, no longer light and floating. My head pounded.

"Iris?" There was a soft knocking. I could barely hear it.

"Iris, honey!"

It was Momma. She was knocking on the bathroom door. I blinked a few times and shivered.

"Yes, Momma?"

"You okay?"

"Yeah," I said, pulling the plug from the drain. "Just a minute!"

I hopped out of the tub and grabbed a towel, half drying myself.

"We won't be going to church this afternoon." Her muffled voice came through the door. I wrapped my-self in the towel and opened the door, letting her in.

"The doctor's office is closed. No way can I get your gran to go to emergency, so Dr. Wringer has agreed to come to the house, bless his heart. He's not sure when. We've got to wait around."

"Yes 'um."

"Well, got you in the bathtub anyway," Momma said.

I nodded and looked at my toes. They were pretty wrinkled.

"Iris?"

I looked up at Momma, afraid, waiting for her to tell me that Gran was dying of some mysterious dis-ease. But she didn't say anything. She just pulled me to her and gave me a big hug, wet towel and all.

"She'll be just fine, honey. She's a strong old gal. A shot of penicillin will put her right in no time." But Momma's voice didn't sound too sure. In fact, it was kind of shaky, like she was trying not to cry.

I shivered and I guess Momma thought I was cold.

"Well, get your clothes back on before *you* catch something," Momma said.

All I could do was nod. I was a nodding fool, afraid to try to say anything.

Chapter Eight

———•———

I took my place, hiding against the dining room wall to listen. It wasn't Dr. Wringer's telling Gran that she probably had viral pneumonia that worried me. I wasn't even overly worried finding out that she had to go in the hospital so they could give her oxygen. After all, I knew Momma would watch over Gran real close at the hospital. What had me worried was the fact that Gran didn't put up much of a fuss. I heard a little whimper, like a kitten, and that was it. Just not like Gran at all.

No one seemed to notice that I was standing in the doorway watching them carry Gran to put her in the car.

"Get the door, Iris" was all anyone said to me.

They laid her down in the backseat of Momma's station wagon.

"I'll meet you folks at the hospital," said the doctor. "Take her through emergency, Carolyn."

Momma and Gramps got in the station wagon and drove off, with the doctor following in his own car. Seemed nobody noticed me standing in the doorway, watching. Maybe they forgot Gran wasn't there to look after me, though they sure should have known it, since

74

she was sprawled across the backseat behind them. Maybe it was my fault Gran was sick; I caused her so much worry. Maybe everybody was mad at me. Then again, maybe it was Ol' Lady Hazard's fault. I wondered again about the tonic Ol' Lady Hazard had been talking about when I saw Gran sneaking out of her house carrying a paper sack.

Maybe if I found that tonic.... I thought on that a minute. How would I know? Would it be in a bottle, or just maybe some strange chopped-up stuff? It could be in any form that would fit in a medium-size paper sack. Gran would probably have hidden it, not wanting Momma to know. I moved around the kitchen, looking in cupboards and drawers. I opened the fridge door for a minute and stared. I pulled open the separate freezer door and peeked inside. Nothing but ice cubes, a quart of boring vanilla ice cream, and some meat and vegetables. It was still clean as a whistle from its recent defrosting and scrub down. Suddenly, the fridge came on with a shudder that made me jump like I was doing something wrong–besides letting all the cold out, which I got yelled at a lot for. I shut the door real quick.

I lifted the lids on Gran's neat and tidy plastic containers, but only found the usual sugar, flour, coffee, macaroni, and stuff. She had tea in the tea tin, like you'd expect. Gran liked her tea. Momma and Gramps were coffee drinkers. Gran said coffee made her jittery. Once Gramps gave me a cup of coffee near white with cream and sugar. Gran had a fit. Said it'd stunt my growth. I wondered if that was why Gramps was a little on the short side.

I moved on to the pantry and looked in the oatmeal box, held the syrup up to the light. It seemed normal enough. I tasted it. Sticky and sweet, like you'd expect. Nothing unusual about the cornstarch, cornflakes, corn syrup, canned corn. I found potatoes in the potato bin and onions in the onion basket. I wondered about going through Gran's drawers in her bedroom, but I would have dropped dead of shame if Gramps had come home and caught me.

I trudged up the stairs to my room, wondering what to do, wondering if Momma would call. I sat on my bed for a minute, got *Silas Marner* off my desk, then stopped dead. My report! I frantically felt my pockets, but it was gone! Then I remembered, I had left my report at the Voodoo Shack! If I was lucky, it would still be sitting on the table. Otherwise, maybe it had already become a part of some mouse nest. I had to get that report back! If I didn't, I would flunk the sixth grade, and that would be the death of Gran, for sure. I wanted to go back to Hazard Swamp then and there to get it, but what if Momma called? What if Gran . . . what if she didn't make it and I was off gallivanting around like I didn't care? I hated that book! I hated it more than Alice Pruitt and her snotty mother, I hated it more than the missing tonic that had poisoned Gran–maybe. I hated myself for causing Gran so much trouble, and most of all, I hated not knowing what to do about any of it. I threw *Silas* against my headboard, feeling a little satisfaction in doing such a bad thing, damaging a book. It landed on its back, the pages fanning slowly, then stopping where the riddle was folded inside.

I felt like a dope. It wasn't the stupid book's fault that things were so messed up. I picked up the book and took the riddle out, trying to ignore it. I read the page the book had fallen open to.

One day, taking a pair of shoes to be mended, he saw the cobbler's wife seated by the fire, suffering from the terrible symptoms of heart–disease and dropsy, which he had witnessed as the precursors of his mother's death. He felt a rush of pity at the mingled sight and remembrance, and, recalling the relief his mother had found from a simple preparation of foxglove, he promised Sally Oats to bring her something that would ease her, since the doctor did her no good.

I worried that Dr. Wringer would do Gran no good. I remembered Gran saying that there was something else that would put her right as rain, and it wasn't drugstore medicine. Maybe it was the antidote to Ol' Lady Hazard's poison.

I picked up the riddle/treasure map/enigma thing and read it again.

Go thru the bog and into the logs
And youl find what I have did.
Think like a buck and youl have sum luck
To find where the treasure is hid.

If I could find the money and turn it over to Ol' Lady Hazard, maybe she would undo her spell on Gran. But the riddle was pure mumbo jumbo.

After what seemed like hours, the telephone rang. I near killed myself racing down the steps to catch it.

"Hello?"

"Iris, it's me," Momma said.

"Momma! How's Gran, is she okay?"

"She's . . . resting comfortably, honey. I'm sorry we left you home all alone. You're probably fit to be tied. Everything happened so fast."

"I'm fine, Momma. I can be alone for a while."

"Of course you can, sweetie."

"How long before Gran can come home?" I asked.

Momma sighed and the phone line was quiet for what seemed a long time. "We'll just have to see."

"She's not going to . . . Well, she's going to be okay, isn't she, Momma?" My voice sounded like I was begging rather than asking.

"I–Well, of course, hon. This kind of pneumonia doesn't respond well . . . they just have to keep trying things. . . ." Momma didn't sound sure. Didn't sound sure at all.

"Can I see her?" I swiped at my eyes.

Momma paused a long time, like she was thinking. "Not today, Iris. Maybe tomorrow."

Would tomorrow be too late? I had to find out what would put Gran right before it was too late; what she was mumbling about before she was carted off to the hospital. Was it something to do with Ol' Lady

Hazard? Or was it me? Had Gran been driven to her bed from having to deal with the likes of me, sneaking out to Hazard Swamp, slurping my spaghetti, and asking troublesome questions all the time? Maybe if I went away. But where?

Suddenly I felt alone and afraid in a big empty house.

"When will you and Gramps be home?" My voice was all wobbly.

I heard Momma take a deep breath. "That was the next thing I was going to talk to you about, Iris. I think I'll stay the night with your Gran, and Gramps probably won't be home 'til late. I have spoken with Tobey's mother, and she insists that you come to their house, have a nice supper, and spend the night."

My brain was screaming NO! but all I said was, "Yes 'um."

"Can you ride your bicycle over? Mrs. Koklemeyer says that she can pick you up if–"

"That's okay. I can ride my bike." My ears were burning hot. Why the Tobster's house? I would likely be the next person rushed off to the hospital, after having to breathe all those fumes from his cologne.

The headlines would read:

CHILD HAS PERMANENT BRAIN DAMAGE—OVERDOSE OF OLD SPICE BLAMED!

"That's a good girl. Now pack a little overnight bag. Toothbrush . . . take your own towel and washcloth, we don't want to impose any more than we have to. Get a clean nightgown–not that ratty old one. Take the new one from last Christmas."

I hardly ever wore the nightgown Momma was telling me to take, because it prickled. I liked my old faded nightgown with the shriveled–up lace, missing buttons, and lopsided bows. I couldn't make it through the night in the new one. It would be sheer torture.

CHILD DIES FROM ITCHING NIGHTGOWN!

"Can you carry the bag okay on your bicycle, honey?"

"Yes, Momma. I'll use some rope."

"There's a good girl."

I heard some muffled talking, like Momma had her hand over the phone.

"Gramps says to please feed Gran's chickens before you go and make sure Sweetums has plenty of hay and fresh water."

"Okay."

"Gotta go, honey. I'll stop and get you at the Koklemeyers' in the morning."

"Can I–can I see Gran then?"

Another long pause, then all's Momma said was: "We'll see."

"Okay."

We hung up and I stared at the phone for a minute. It was bad enough Gran was sick, why did I have to go to the Tobster's? Was I being punished?

I packed my overnight bag, then went to the chicken yard and scattered some feed.

"Here, chick chick chick."

It wasn't really necessary to call Gran's prize chickens. Every time they saw a person, they scurried about, cackling and running in circles. The rooster—we called him Popinjay—strutted around, his combs jiggling like Jell-O. I always found chickens a mite dumb, but Gran thought the world of her hens. When one of them would quit laying, Gran would get real quiet, and her lips would tighten up.

"We'll give her a couple of more days. Maybe she's just off her scratch," Gran would say.

"She's past her prime. You want me to do it?" Gramps would ask.

We all knew what was going to happen. Gran would never let Gramps do the butchering. She didn't trust him to make a clean job of it.

The next Sunday we would have stewed chicken. We all hated stewed chicken.

"Quit givin' them names and making them pets," Gramps once said.

"What about that old mule of yours?" Gran had snapped back. "When's the last time he earned his keep? Don't see you putting a gun to his head."

"Mule's different. Besides, who ever heard of eating a mule?"

"Humph," Gran had said.

I went into the chicken coop and collected the eggs. Momma had forgotten to ask me to do that, maybe because it was my regular chore. I got an even dozen.

Marybeth's nesting box was empty. Looked like she wasn't doing her job anymore. I sure wasn't gonna be the one to tell Gran the news.

Sweetums was taking his afternoon nap in the shade of a lean–to attached to the barn. There was an open bale of hay inside the barn. I sorted out two leaves and tossed them into the feeder, then filled the water trough.

I tied my suitcase onto the rack on my back bicycle fender and headed for the Koklemeyer House of Horrors. I hoped with all my heart that Mrs. Koklemeyer would not make me eat something I hated, like squash or liver. I was almost to the Koklemeyer house when my heart skipped a beat after I remembered my book report, still sitting on the table in the clubhouse. I had to go and get it, plain and simple as that. Maybe at least Tobey would help me finish the darn thing. I hoped I could remember how to get to the Voodoo Shack through the woods at the end of Tobey's street. I would have to hurry, that was for sure, because it was starting to get dark and it looked like it might rain again.

I was thinking about what the night had in store at the Koklemeyers'. I looked down the street at the Tobster's innocent–looking house. Little did the world know that inside lurked things too horrible to mention. I really wanted to be home with Gran and Momma and Gramps, sitting around the dinner table, Gran with her eye on me, like always, making sure I used my napkin instead of my sleeve.

I squeezed my eyes shut, hoping that I would wake up and everything would be right and normal. Instead I got: "Hey, Iris, what's goin' on?"

Greenie Skinner was tooling up on his beat–up bicycle. He hopped off and let it drop on the sidewalk with a crash. No wonder the paint was all scratched and the fenders bent up.

I told Greenie about my Gran being sick, and about my book report, and my fate–worse–than–death at the Koklemeyers'. He put his arm around my shoulder, gave me a squeeze, and said he felt right sorry. It felt good, the squeeze.

"So, I've got to go get my book report, then get back here in time for supper at the Tobster's."

"Gee, Iris, I'd get it for you, but me and Pa are just fixin' to leave for a fishing trip. Hope it don't rain," he added, looking at the darkening sky. "I'll tell Pa about your gran. She'll be fit as a fiddle. You'll see."

I nodded, but I wasn't convinced.

"I'll bring you some pan fish," he said, hopping back on his old bike.

That would be good. Gran liked fried fish. So did Gramps. I would even clean them without complaining.

Thunder growled in the distance.

Rain. That was all I needed.

Chapter Nine

———•———

Gramps always said that a bad plan was worse than no plan at all. Going for my homework with a storm coming was a bad plan. The thunder was getting steadily louder. I could see flashes of lightning through the trees. I was getting all turned around and got off the main path a couple of times. I wished I had paid more attention when the Tobster and I had gone before. I rode my bike down the path a ways, but it kept getting bogged down in the mud. Once I fell over and got my pants all muddy. So I left my bike leaning against a big oak tree, which I hoped would make it easier to find, and hung my overnight bag from the handlebars.

I came to another fork. Which way had the Tobster and I gone before? I took the more worn-looking path. I was sure I'd gone miles—maybe on the wrong path. I was wearing my good shoes, too, and the walk was not doing them any good.

A clap of thunder seemed to shake the trees. I speeded up. I decided to forget my book report, maybe just rewrite it. That's what I should have done to begin with. I turned and looked back the way I had come.

Then things got worse. The sky got ugly, fast, and the wind came up. The trees creaked and groaned as they swayed back and forth. The cold cut through my lightweight jacket. I ran, my feet slipping, branches slapping my face, and brambles snatching my pant legs. The rain poured through the leafless trees, dripping from my nose, and soaking my clothes.

I scrunched my chin into my chest, watching the path through eye slits. My feet sloshed along the muddy path. Suddenly there was nothing under my foot when I stepped. I tripped, twisting as I fell. I'd tripped in a hole and was sitting in a sea of mud. I got myself untwisted and stood up, testing my ankle. It hurt some, but I could walk. I was caked with mud and my wrists burned with scrapes.

When I looked up from my scraped wrists, I saw it: the Voodoo Shack! Of course! I had fallen in one of Ol' Lady Hazard's treasure–digging holes. I gimped over to the woodshed, got the key from behind the no-trespassing sign, then scrambled over to the cabin. Just as I reached to unlock the door, a crash of thunder about scared me out of my wits.

My heart hammered in my ears when I pushed the key into the padlock and turned it. The door creaked and I peeked inside. I had never been to the cabin alone, especially that late. My book report still sat on the table. I picked it up and put it in my soggy shirt pocket. The cabin was cold as a meat locker but at least it was dry. Or fairly dry. Rain ran down one cabin wall in a little stream. More water came through the roof and puddled on the cracked cement floor.

I sat down at the table and fumbled around in my pockets, looking for leftover poker matches. I quickly lit the lantern. The cold began to creep into me, and pretty soon I was shivering. My belly growled. I looked at my watch. It was six–thirty. Probably the Koklemeyers were sitting around the supper table. I imagined a plate set for me, heaped with steaming hot food. Even liver and squash would be okay.

They would wonder why I hadn't showed up. Maybe they would think I was waiting out the rain. I wondered if Mrs. Koklemeyer would drive over to my house to look for me.

The Tobster would be pouting, poking at his food, thinking I had stood him up.

"Now, Tobias, eat your supper," his mother would say nervously, wringing her hands. "I'm sure she'll be here." She would call our phone number at the house, but it would ring and ring with no answer.

My rumbling stomach was drowned out by the sound of my teeth chattering. I didn't even have a blanket, let alone a sleeping bag. I sat dripping, adding another puddle to the floor, while the wind howled.

I couldn't go home *or* to the Koklemeyers', because of the storm. It would be completely dark soon, and I would *never* find my way out of the woods. Besides, my ankle was throbbing like it wanted to explode. That meant I would have to stay at the Voodoo Shack. What I needed was a fire. I looked at the old potbellied stove crouched in the corner.

I went over to it real cautious, reached out, and pulled open a little door in front. It screeched like it needed oil, and a mouse jumped out, nearly scaring the pants off me. A fire poker stood next to the stove. I picked it up and dug around inside the stove in the shredded paper, checking for more mice.

I knew from our fireplace at home that the flue had to be opened before a fire was lit. I found a lever on the pipe and turned it. Now I needed something to burn.

Firewood. Of course! The woodshed out back; us kids had explored it once. It was loaded with chunks of firewood. I stood at the doorway for a minute, watching the rain blow around, then made a mad dash.

The rain whipped me like a lazy mule. When I hobbled through the woodshed door, I was near smothered with enough cobwebs to stuff a mattress. I waited a few seconds for my eyes to adjust to the dark.

I stepped up to a mound of wood and reached out for a piece. What about varmints? I knew how snakes and rats liked to hide in the woodpiles. If a rattler got me, who would know? It might be years before anyone would find my bones, picked clean by ants and worms. I mustered my courage and grabbed a piece. No poisonous snakes, no rabid rats. I snatched another and another, until I was loaded up, then limped as fast as I could back to the cabin.

I pushed the door open, staggered to the stove, and dumped the wood into a heap. It was old and powdery dry, and would probably burn fast. I knew I would need to bring in a lot more to last the night. First things first: light the fire.

I'd never used a potbellied stove before, but I had

helped Gramps set fires in the big stone fireplace at the house. Iris the Pyro, Momma called me.

I stuffed a couple of logs in on top of the aban-doned mouse nests. Next I managed to get another match going and tossed it into the stove. It flickered and fizzled out. Darn! Only a couple of matches left. I added a couple of more sticks of wood, lit another match, and held it to the shredded papers. A tiny flame started, then began to fade and die. I blew a little and it came back to life. I heard a small snap. The snap became a crackle, and the flames grew and spread. Some smoke came out the door, stinging my eyes, but most seemed to go up the stovepipe where it belonged. I added another piece of wood. There was only one more left after that. I would have to make a million trips back to the woodshed, with a bum ankle.

A little heat was beginning to rise from the stove. I rubbed my hands together over the top, feeling the warmth. I lifted each foot close to the stove until steam began to rise from my ruined good shoes.

When I tried to open the stove door, I burnt my hand pretty good. I blew on my scorched fingers and shook my hand. Now I had a burnt hand and a twisted ankle. I decided it was a good time to bring in enough wood to last the night. The wind had eased some, but the rain still came down in sheets as I made trip after trip. I quit when my ankle gave out. I opened the door of the stove, this time using the hook on the end of the poker. The fire was lively. I threw in another log, which burst into flames when it hit the coals. My watch said it was almost eight thirty. I couldn't believe it was so late!

The rain had not let up, and the wind rattled the front door like it wanted in where it was warm.

I yawned and sat on the slat bedsprings of the lower bunk. Best thing to do, I decided, was to get to sleep and get up real early, hike back down the path, and find my bike. Maybe I could sneak back to the house, say that I was afraid to leave because of the storm. I was in the basement, like I'd been taught to do when it stormed bad, and didn't hear the phone. It would be an out-and-out fib, but I couldn't tell where I'd spent the night.

I went over to the stove and crammed in a half dozen pieces of wood, hoping they would last the night. I stretched out on the bare metal strips of the bed, feeling them cut into me. My hair snagged every time I moved.

About that time, the lantern dimmed, flickered, and went out. After the last of the glow died, it was as dark as the inside of Jonah's whale. There was only a small light coming through slats on the woodstove.

I lay wide awake for what seemed hours, thinking some about my throbbing ankle and burnt hand, but mostly thinking about Gran, maybe dying, in a hospital bed. I tried to ignore the sound of the door rattling in the wind and the water running off the roof, but the noises bounced around in my head, seeming louder as the hours crawled by. I stared into the dark, watching shadows twist and squirm on the ceiling. My stomach had another grumbling fit, then eased up. I had to go to the bathroom, but far as I could tell, there wasn't a Texaco station nearby. I stumbled through the dark until I found the door, squatted at the edge of the porch to go, and then quickly groped my way back inside.

I checked the fire one more time. When I opened the door to the stove, it was so hot I could barely chuck any more wood in. I lay back down on my miserable bed, closed my eyes, and wished I could sleep so the worst night of my life would end.

Chapter Ten

It was pitch-dark. My lungs burned. Smoke was everywhere—thick, choking. Fire! I leapt off the bunk and plunged into the darkness like a blind person. I looked for the door, hurrying. I couldn't breathe. I remembered what I'd learned in school: that there'd be less smoke down low. I dropped to my hands and knees and crawled. The air was a little better, but I still had trouble breathing.

I smacked my head on something—a chair. I turned and continued to crawl, then slammed into something else—maybe a counter. I gave up crawling and scooted on my bottom, my eyes swollen shut, coughing, choking. It was sweltering. I managed to open one eye a little. Something glowed cherry red in front of me. Had to be the stove; the smoke was thicker around it.

I scooted backward, trying to concentrate. I felt a wall behind me and followed it. I kept inching my way along the wall, then heard it. A rattle. The wonderful glorious rattle of the door! My heart jumped when I felt a little cold trickle of air. I crouched, then stood, feeling with both hands until I found it: the doorknob!

I jerked the door open and staggered onto the porch, gulping air.

I forced my rubbery legs to take me off the porch to the edge of the woods. The sun was trying to come up, but was mostly blotted by clouds. I turned to look at the cabin. Thick smoke poured out the chimney and through cracks in one wall.

A freight train roared through my head. I was falling, falling, twirling like a whirligig from a maple tree. I heard a voice; it grunted. Someone pulled me, then lifted me onto something hard. I dreamed I was riding in a wheelbarrow, at least I expect it was a dream. Nothing else made sense. Then there was more lifting and hands pulling me, then a sharp voice commanding me to walk. I fell onto something soft . . . like a bed.

I wondered if it was raining. I could feel wet on my face. I opened my eyes, but everything was blurry. Slowly I focused on two sets of eyes looking at me. One set was brown, the other green. The brown ones belonged to a woman's face, and she was trying to smother me with a cloth. I hollered and pushed her hand away, then snapped upright.

"Take it easy!" she said.

I rubbed my fists in my eyes and blinked. I near jumped out of my skin when I saw her face. It was the neon orange lipstick that gave me a start. She had her eyelids smeared up with bright blue eye shadow, and wore earrings big enough to double as wind chimes. Who was she? I fought to clear the cobwebs out of my head. When she leaned away from me a little and I got a good view, I finally recognized her. It was Ol' Lady Hazard!

"What...where..." I said, looking around. I was sitting on a couch.

Ol' Lady Hazard stood in front of me, holding a cloth, probably full of chloroform or something. Her big jingly earrings made little tinkling noises every time she moved. Her hair was kind of stringy, dark with gray streaks, and hung in a loose ponytail down to her shoulders. She wore real ugly bright orange pants–to go with the orange lipstick, I guess–and a yellow shirt, both a little too tight. A half dozen bracelets and maybe as many strings of beads clinked and swayed when she moved. She didn't *look* like a witch, exactly, but she was surely a sight!

An ink black cat sat perched on the back of the couch, staring at me with those green eyes. The room was none too clean and chock–full of plants and bottles and jars. Every inch of space on the tables and floor was covered with knickknacks and gewgaws, doilies, cups, plates, statues, lamps with fringy shades, pictures, stuffed animals (once alive, now dead), and tons of dusty junk like you'd try to sell off at the church bazaar.

I scrunched against the back of the couch. It was covered with a turquoise–and–lime–green blanket. The springs poked my bottom from underneath. I stared at Ol' Lady Hazard, and she looked back at me.

"You're the Weston girl, ain't cha?" she said.

I sat dumb as a rock, staring at her cloth.

"Well, ain't cha?"

"Yeah–yes 'um."

"Thought so. I know yer granny."

I nodded, my voice temporarily out of order.

Ol' Lady Hazard jingle–jangled out of the room and disappeared into the kitchen. It looked to be in a worse state than the living room. Her back was to me. Now was my chance to escape! I jumped off the couch, but before I could take two steps the room started spinning, making me plunk right back down. She'd drugged me for sure! I heard clinking noises come from the kitchen.

I tried to get up again, slower. The cat hissed at me, its pupils going bigger then smaller.

"Luther, leave the girl alone!" shouted Ol' Lady Hazard from the kitchen.

How did she know, so far away and with her back to us?

She came back from the kitchen carrying a chipped coffee mug, which she shoved at me. "Drink," she commanded.

I took it, holding it as far away as possible. I'd eat worms before I'd put it to my lips. Steam rose from the mug, carrying a sweetish, minty aroma. It didn't smell bad, but what witch worth her salt would make a poison drink smell like . . . well, poison?

"It's my special mix," she said. "Drink up."

You bet it was special. I thought about tossing it in her face, and making a run for it. My head was starting to clear, and I had it in the back of my mind that maybe I could find out the truth, the "burden" she'd passed along to Gran. The tonic. What about the tonic?

Think, Iris, think. I glanced around the room, hoping a clue would pop out at me.

"I–I'll let it cool a little," I said, just as smooth as silk, setting the mug on a tiny patch of open space available on an end table.

Ol' Lady Hazard plunked down next to me, her jewelry rattling on impact. I felt myself stiffen, trying to get ready for . . . whatever. I suppose I reeked, all smoke and sweat, but she had an odor on her that was like nothing I'd ever smelled. It wasn't bad, just strange, like onion grass, catnip, and something sweet–maybe a little perfume–all rolled together.

"What's yer first name, girl? Can't fer the life uh me remember."

"Um–Iris."

She snapped her fingers. "That's right, Iris Weston. I reckon yer ma's wondering where you got to."

Momma! She must be near crazy with worry.

"Could I use your phone, please? I need to call my mother."

"Use tuh have one of those things, but they took it."

"Well, then, I should be going. I–"

"I ain't through with you yet, girl. You know I hauled you all the way here in my wheelbarrow. Ain't got a car. You're none too light for an old lady to be luggin' around."

So I had been riding in a wheelbarrow! I thought it was a dream.

"Almost didn't go a'tall, doncha know. I thought I smelled smoke and I asked myself how in blazes anything could be burnin' with all that rain. Must be imaginin' things. Then, 'bout daybreak, I see the smoke.... Well, anyway, you hungry?"

"Huh? Oh, no, I–" My stomach growled–traitor!

"If you got yer legs back, girl, come into the kitchen and we'll see if we can getcha a little somethin'."

I wobbled after her, my ankle still giving me fits. I felt like a condemned person taking her final walk. I tried not to stare when I walked into the kitchen. The windowsills and countertops were jammed with plants and weeds, twisted and stalky. Strange smells churned in the air, making a funny taste in my mouth. I scanned the room for a door. There was one, but it was blocked by a huge, potted tree–like thing with scant few leaves.

The kitchen table was covered with newspapers and had dried–up plants and stems strung all over. There were two chairs at the table, and I slipped into one. I kept my hands in my lap and my elbows off the table, afraid to touch anything.

Ol' Lady Hazard plunked a bowl of something–soup, I guess–in front of me. I smelled garlic, that was for sure, but anything else she'd stirred in there was a mystery.

"Now, you ain't leavin' here 'til you et this up," she said.

The black cat sauntered into the room and jumped on the table, giving me a start. It fixed those green eyes on me, then sniffed my soup. A pink tongue slipped in and out of its mouth as it lapped from the bowl.

"Luther! Bad cat," said Ol' Lady Hazard, taking a swipe at him. He jumped from the table to the cupboard and wound his way through the junk on the countertop. I figured it was a good sign, having the cat taste my soup. Someone had told me once that you can never poison a cat; they're much too smart.

I lifted the spoon to my lips, trying not to slurp. She banged down a plate with a couple of slices of bread. It looked like the basic Wonder Bread that Gran always bought. I'd never heard of anybody being poisoned by bread and I *was* pretty hungry. So far, the soup concoction was sitting all right in my belly. Ol' Lady Hazard watched me eat. I tried to use my best table manners and not slurp. When the spoon clanked into the empty bowl, I mopped the last drops with my bread crust and stuffed it in my mouth.

"Feelin' better?" she asked.

"Yes–um, if you'll 'scuse me, I really should go–"

"Hold yer horses, Iris. I got a question."

I stared at my lap and began to poke at the blisters starting on my hand, wishing I'd slipped out when I'd had the chance.

"What in blue blazes where you doing at that old cabin, child, on a stormy night? You run away from home?"

I shrugged to the first question, and shook my head to the second.

"S'matter? Cat got yer tongue? Were ya there on some kinda dare, or somethin'?"

"No, ma'am, I just went there to . . . Well, I left something there."

"Now, what would you leave there? You go there regular, do ya?"

I thought maybe the soup *was* poison, because my stomach was beginning to flip-flop.

She didn't wait for the answer to that question before she shot off another one: "How'd you expect to be gone all night and not be missed?"

I told her the story, about my gran, about the Koklemeyers, and how it had stormed and I got cold and built a fire.

"I'd heard your granny had taken sick. Didn't know she'd gone in the hospital." Then she kind of muttered something under her breath about not getting the mixture right.

"Built a fire in that old stove, did ya?"

"Yes 'um. Now, if you don't mind, I really do have to find my mother," I said, rising from my chair.

"Not so fast!" she snapped, pushing me back. "When'd you find Bill's hunting cabin?"

"I–I was just taking a walk and came across it. We–I go there sometimes, to, ah, think."

"Think, huh?" She scratched her chin a little, and tightened up her orange lips.

"Well, some of us kids go there sometimes," I mumbled. Didn't seem much reason to keep the club a secret anymore, since I figured the Voodoo Shack was probably nothing but a pile of ashes.

Ol' Lady Hazard clucked her tongue and shook her head, setting those earrings to tinkling. "I thought it looked like somebody'd been there. I never figured it to be a bunch of kids. I wish you'd done it right, though, and burned it up. I hate that cabin. Hate it!"

She was becoming agitated, pacing the room. The black cat hopped off the counter and wound around her ankles. I thought about making a dash for it. I was pretty sure I could outrun her, even with my bum ankle. But I just sat there, like I was glued to my chair.

"Luther–scoot!" she snapped. The cat jumped on the table next to me and sniffed my empty bowl. He looked at me and squeezed his eyes shut, real slow. I half expected to see him turn into a frog or something.

"It–it didn't burn down, then?" I asked.

"'Fraid not, blast it all. Logs were probably too soggy from all the rain. A lot of smoke. You musta had one dandy fire going."

I nodded again, then kind of stood up, crouching a little so's maybe she wouldn't notice.

"Still don't make sense to me, goin' all the way out there alone like that. Place gives me the spooks," she said. She hugged herself like she was cold all of a sudden. "Your granny's in Harley Memorial, I expect."

"I–I guess," I said, working my way backward, still crouched down some.

"You guess, do you? Why you being so edgy, child? Anyone spends the night in that cabin's gotta be gutsy. What's her room number?"

"Room number?" I sounded like a parrot.

"Yeah! Yer granny's room number–at the hospital."

"Don't know. Um, I haven't been there."

Then Ol' Lady Hazard's face softened up a bit, and she smiled. I inched backward some more. My back was starting to ache, so I straightened up a little.

"Always called her Sissy, your gran. She hates her name, Harriet, so I called her Sissy. I recall helping her out once."

Sissy? Like in sister. What was Ol' Lady Hazard talking about anyway, with helping her out?

Then she looked at me real hard, so I crouched again, like I was sitting in the chair–except by now it was a good three feet away. If she noticed that I was sitting like some mime on a pretend chair, she didn't mention it.

"It was about yer ma, I remember. Sissy was fit to be tied, she was. Yep, yer ma was overseas in Korea and yer granny had herself whipped into a frenzy. I got her turned around, though."

I sat–crouched real quiet for a minute, trying to remember Gran's words when they carted her off to the hospital. Something about not needing drugstore medicine, that something had made her right as rain when she was sick with worry, back when Momma was in Korea.

"I don't expect your momma would take kindly to my medicine, her being a nurse and all. I fancy myself as a nurse of sorts, too," she said, smoothing an imaginary wrinkle out of her blouse. "Well, anyway, the devil with it. I ain't saying it's magic or anything." She picked up my empty bowl and carried it to the sink. She paused a minute to give me a funny look. I couldn't pretend-sit any longer, so I just kind of bent over. "But them days is gone, now that my special book is lost."

Special book? I knew it! I'd bet anything she was talking about some witchcraft book. I backed up and leaned, casual-like, against the door jamb. I looked at my fingernails. They were pretty dirty.

"Book?" I said, using my smooth voice.

"Yeah. I call it my bible. Dang husband of mine hid it somewheres. 'Course, he can't tell me where he hid it *now*, can he?"

"No, ma'am."

"He always liked playing with me, ya know. Not nice, mind, but nasty, like a cat plays with a mouse. Blast his soul. 'Course you heard about him dying: I expect he's in a hot place now. Well, he was a mean one, 'specially when he drank too much—which was all the time."

"Yes, 'um."

"But he's gone now, and I ain't none too sad. I still get his disability check, which was the only thing he was good fer. Leastwise to me." She gave out a little cackle, which made my skin crawl. "But I need my special book back, and I'm fit to be tied lookin' for it."

She turned to look at me, then just like that, she went into one of those trances. When her eyeballs rolled back into her head, I forgot all about my sore ankle and left so fast it took a half mile for my legs to catch my feet.

Chapter Eleven

———•———

Momma hugged me so hard, I thought I heard a rib or two pop. "I thought I lost you, too," she said.

There were sheriff's cars everywhere, and that's what near ran me over when I was sprinting down the two-track road from Ol' Lady Hazard's. They had found my purple bicycle and my overnight bag, and Momma was sure that I'd been kidnaped by one of those perverts who lurk around the school yards and candy stores. The Koklemeyers had called Momma at the hospital when I didn't show.

It was lucky that Greenie and his pa had ended their fishing trip early because of their sleeping bags and tent getting soaked. When Momma started calling all my friends the next morning, it was Greenie who told where I was headed, to get my book report. *Silas Marner* would be the end of me yet. I knew I could make Greenie Skinner eat worms for telling where the Voodoo Shack was, but right then, feeling Momma squeeze the air out of me, I didn't think so.

I tried to explain, I really did. Momma whisked me

off to the doctor because of the smoke, and then there was my ankle and burnt hand.

Dr. Wringer said my lungs were clear. He gave me a tetanus shot for good measure and wrapped my ankle in an Ace bandage. He gave us some burn salve for my hand.

Next thing, Momma took me home and marched me up to the tub. Once Gramps had gotten word that I was found in one piece, he did some chores and went back to the hospital. I wished he had been home when I got there. I always felt a little better when Gramps was around. I asked Momma how Gran was. All she said was, "Holdin' her own."

I took my bath and put on clean clothes. When I came downstairs, scrubbed clean, and woozy from lack of sleep, I found Momma in the kitchen making me a bacon–and–egg sandwich. She wasn't talking much, but she was making a lot of noise with the cast–iron skillet. I guess she had gone from being relieved to being mad. I chewed my sandwich while Momma slammed and clanged her way around the kitchen. After a while, I couldn't stand it anymore.

"Momma?"

She whirled around to face me, ponytail slapping and hands on her hips. I stopped chewing and stared at a scratch in the tabletop.

"Well, what is it, Iris?" Momma snapped.

"I . . ."

Her foot began to tap, just like Gran's. I wondered if foot tapping was a Weston family trait, too.

"I'm . . . sorry. I didn't mean to cause so much trouble. It's just . . . I . . ."

Momma softened some and sat at the table with me. She lifted my chin and made me look at her. "Why couldn't you just have gone straight to Tobey's?"

Momma looked a lot older than last time I'd seen her. She wasn't wearing any lipstick, and a good amount of her hair had come loose from its rubber band. A big knot in my throat stopped any words from coming out.

"Iris, I just wouldn't have anything to live for if something happened to you. Your gran–she's old, and . . . we have to prepare . . . then there's all the bills that'll be coming. I can't even think about those. . . ."

"Gran? She's going to be all right, isn't she, Momma?" I kept asking that question, hoping for an answer. And I'd never thought about the bills, for the hospital and all.

"I–I just don't know, honey. But she's asking for you, and I'm going to take you over to the hospital. Anybody asks, tell them that you're thirteen."

By now my shoulders had begun to do a jittery little dance. Tears plopped on my bacon-and-egg sandwich. Then the floodgates opened and I thought I might wash my sandwich clean off the table with the tears and snot running all over the place.

Momma started to cry, too, and handed me a wad of napkins. I wiped my face, blew my nose, and took in a big gulp of air.

Then she started to giggle, which I thought was peculiar. Then she was giggling and crying. "Iris, remember that kid in the drugstore, playing around with the paper napkin holder, then shooting napkins all over the place when Mrs. Pruitt yelled at him about the paper plates?"

Momma was laughing now and shredding a napkin into little pieces. She was scaring me, but for some reason I couldn't help but laugh, too.

"Yes, Momma, and Alice–*Allison*–had to use baby paper plates for her la–de–da party. Momma?"

She was dabbing her red eyes with a piece of napkin. "Ye–yes, Iris?"

"What's that club Mrs. Pruitt was talking about?"

"Oh, Iris, it has to do with tracing your family back a few generations."

Momma had quieted down some, but still giggled now and then. "You know what I heard, honey?"

"What, Momma?"

"I heard that Roberta Pruitt– No, I really shouldn't tell you. It's not right."

"What? Tell me," I begged.

"Well, what the hey. You know Mrs. Whip, Randy's mother?"

"Yes, 'um."

"Well, I really shouldn't gossip."

"Momma!"

She dropped her voice real low, like someone was right around the corner listening. "Mrs. Whip says she and Randy were at the pawnshop. Evidently, Randy has his heart set on one of those awful electric guitars. Well, anyway, Mrs. Whip said that she saw Roberta Pruitt there and she was pawning her good china."

"Pawning?"

"That's when you sell it cheap to get some quick cash, then try to raise the money to buy it back. After so many days, if you don't claim it, then the pawn-broker–the shop owner–can sell it."

"Oh. How come?"

"For the money, of course," Momma said.

"But the way Alice talks, they have tons of money."

"Well, sweetie, I guess not. Now, I'm not saying I'm glad that Roberta has fallen on hard times. Must be Dr. Pruitt wasn't in good financial shape when he passed away. It's just that she's so . . ."

"Stuck–up?" I offered.

"Yes. She has no right saying things . . . telling folks lies. Well, now I'm no better than her, and I'm ashamed. Lord knows we might have to pawn some things for the doctor bill."

Now there was more to worry about besides whether Gran would get better. Now Momma was worried about the doctor bill. I wondered if Gran was worried, too. That was something she didn't need.

Momma got up, poured herself a cup of coffee, got me a glass of chocolate milk, and sat back down at the table. She took a deep breath and pulled herself up straight. "Now, Iris Mae Weston, you're going to tell me all about this place. . . ."

"What place, Momma?" I knew darn well what place she was asking about.

"That old cabin Greenie sent us to, when we were looking for you–where you left your homework. I want to know what it is that you do there and with whom. I've figured out it's the reason you disappear every so often."

So I told Momma about it being a clubhouse for us kids. How we just messed around, told stories, and played games. I didn't tell her about the game being poker, though, or about the cookies that I ate, sometimes spoiling my supper.

Momma looked at me real hard, deciding if I was telling the truth. She didn't have the built-in lie detector that Gran had—yet. Besides, I wasn't fibbing, just maybe glossing things over a bit.

"You're not gonna tell Gran, are you?" I said.

"Heavens no! She's asking about you, sure nobody's taking proper care of you. It will be Christmas in July before we ever tell her about this place you go and what happened last night. I want you to wear your corduroys with the hem let out so that Ace bandage doesn't show, and if she notices your hand, tell her you forgot to use a potholder."

I finished my milk.

"So, who belongs to this club?"

I looked in my empty glass. "Well, Greenie, of course, and the Tob—er, Tobey, Cecilia Campbell, and Randy. That's about it. Alice Pruitt wants in."

Momma looked at me real close. "You going to let her in?"

I shook my head.

"Iris, I don't want you telling the other kids about Mrs. Pruitt going to the pawn shop. Mrs. Whip said that Randy has been told not to repeat this. You and he are not to discuss it, hear? Just remember next time that Alice is hurtful toward you, that she is no better than you or anybody else."

"Yes, Momma."

"Well, enough said."

I got up and carried our dishes to the sink. I started to roll up my sleeves.

"They'll keep," Momma said.

They had Gran under a clear plastic tent that was supposed to help her breathe. Momma unzipped it and pulled a corner back so we could talk a little. Gran was near white as the sheet she lay on, and black smudges circled under her eyes. Her hair was in a braid instead of a bun and loose strands stuck out everywhere. She reached out her hand and I could see blue veins through the skin.

"Iris," Gran said, her voice croaky.

"Hi," I said.

We smiled at each other and held hands.

"How you feelin'?" I asked.

"I've been better, honey."

She coughed a little, then looked me up and down.

"Well, looks like you've at least been behavin' yourself."

Momma seemed to have a little choking fit, then muttered something about going to find the doctor. I looked at the bottle hanging from a rack next to Gran's bed. A tube ran off it down under the covers. I knew it was dripping something into her arm. My stomach gave a little turn when I thought about the needle.

A nurse came in, her starchy uniform crackling. She was shaking a thermometer and looking at it.

"How are we today?" asked the nurse.

"Humph," Gran said.

The nurse continued to smile and stuck the thermometer in Gran's mouth. Next she wheeled over a gadget that looked like a giant thermometer and wrapped the band part of the gizmo around Gran's arm. She pumped on a little rubber ball a few times. Something hissed like the air was coming out of a tire and the nurse clucked as she took the band off Gran's arm. Next she snatched the thermometer out of Gran's mouth. We watched the nurse scowl at the thermometer for a minute, shake it down, and put it in a tube of alcohol. Still scowling, she took a pen out of her pocket and wrote on a clipboard hanging at the end of Gran's bed. Finally, the nurse bustled out and we were alone.

It was the first time I felt like I was stronger than Gran. Seemed like it took every ounce of strength for her to just take in air. Her hand lay limp in mine. I didn't have to be a rocket scientist to know that Gran was slipping.

Gran turned her head a little and faced me. Her eyes were dull and it seemed she wasn't looking at me at all.

"You being a good girl?" she whispered.

I nodded.

"Fool doctors . . . not helping me, need Missy's potion." Her eyes closed.

"Gran!" My heart thumped like mad.

Slowly her lids opened.

"Gran. You gave me a start."

"I should sleep now, Iris. Bring–Missy–here . . ."

Missy? Who the heck was Missy? Maybe one of her chickens. What would she want one of her chickens for?

"Gran, who's Missy?"

"Is it Easter yet?" she said, her voice barely a whisper.

"No, Gran, tomorrow. Gran, who's Missy?"

"Put in a good word or two for me at church. . . ." Her voice trailed off and she closed her eyes again. I saw her chest was rising and falling regular.

I told her I surely would.

Chapter Twelve

Gran had asked me to put in a word for her at Easter service, but we didn't go because Momma and Gramps didn't want to leave Gran alone too long. I had gone to the hospital for a little while. Gran never woke up when I was in her room. She mumbled some words a couple of times about that Missy person. I figured she was delirious. I sat in a chair next to her bed. I prayed, hoping it was okay with God that I wasn't in church. It seemed like forever that I sat on that chair, staring at my gran . . . except it wasn't her, wasn't her at all.

I got up and slid into the hall. I wasn't old enough to be visiting, but nobody made anything of it, especially since Momma worked there and all. I saw her and Gramps sitting in a little waiting area that had been decorated with Easter bunnies and such. Momma was leaning forward with her elbows on her knees, and Gramps was holding his head in his hands. I heard Momma tell Gramps not to worry, first things first. Gramps said that Gran was everything to him, and he'd sell the farm if that would make her well again. I wondered what he was talking about, selling the farm. Next to Gran, I knew he loved the farm more than anything. It had been in the family for several of those generations that the Pruitts were fussing about. Then it dawned on me. It was the money! Gran had been in the hospital for going on three days. I reckoned her bill was up to hundreds of dollars, maybe more. Maybe lots more.

I went back to Gran's room, but was too fidgety to sit. After a while, Momma came in and said that Gramps would run me home. She took over the chair next to Gran's bed. Gramps didn't say much on the drive home. He sat all crumpled behind the steering wheel. He said Dr. Wringer was trying a new antibiotic. If that didn't work, then they would try something else. He didn't sound like he held much hope, though.

After Gramps dropped me off, I went to my room and lay on my bed, staring at the stain on my ceiling. It had a top hat and sort of a beard and reminded me of Abraham Lincoln. Nobody could see it but me.

It didn't seem like Easter Sunday. No smell of ham baking, no kitchen noises from Gran and Momma banging around getting things ready. Gramps would usually make a big deal out of sharpening the carving knife. It was his job to slice the ham or turkey or roast, depending on the occasion. But the kitchen was empty, the countertops clean, except where I'd had some cereal and left the bowl in the sink. Wasn't much sense in washing one stupid bowl and spoon.

I tried to work on my *Silas Marner* book report, but it was no use. The book was print-side down across my stomach as I lay sprawled across my bed, staring at Abe.

Now there was a new worry. Money. Actually, money had always come up in conversations now and then, when someone told me that we couldn't afford something that I wanted, like a new bike. But this was different. This was more serious. Maybe I couldn't make Gran better, but I was darned if Gramps would lose the thing second most important if I could help it. I had near twenty dollars in my savings. Maybe that would help, and I'd sell my bike. That was another five, maybe ten dollars. I'd even baby–sit Mrs. Ribber's kids, the Terrible Twins, and that would make me a few more dollars. I sighed. Who was I kidding? What good was thirty, maybe forty, dollars going to do against a big hospital bill? I needed real money. What was I going to do, rob a gas station?

Then I remembered the stolen money, and the reward us kids had figured on. If I could get everyone to donate their share, it might help some. I *knew* it was somewhere in the Voodoo Shack. It had to be, but where?

I imagined Ol' Man Hazard trying to think of a good hiding place for the stolen dough. Mr. Marner, in the book, had done some thinking about where to hide his gold. Of course, it was stolen anyway and replaced by a little girl named Eppie. Or at least that was the way he saw it, like a gift from God or some-thing. I thought about the riddle we had found, and went over it again and again in my head. The answer was in the riddle, sure as heck.

Go thru the bog and into the logs
And youl find what I have did.

That had to mean going through the swamp into
Hazard Woods. Of course, the cabin was made of logs,
too. Maybe the logs meant the cabin. I knew the treasure was in the cabin–somewhere.

Think like a buck and youl have sum luck
To find where the treasure is hid.

Think like a buck? I closed my eyes. I was tired of
looking at Abe. I wished somebody would paint the
ceiling. It was like that deer head at the cabin, always
there, watching every move, that stupid grin on its
mouth.

I sat up so quick my book flew off my stomach and
clunked on the floor.

It was there all the time staring at me. Think! Like
a buck.

I practically ran all the way to the Voodoo Shack. I
wanted to make sure I would get back before dark. I'd
have rather eaten worms and died than to have spent
another night there. Nobody had bothered to padlock
the door, which stood propped open to air things out. I
hurried inside and was startled by a red squirrel as it
scolded and scampered past.

The cabin, though never much to look at, was really
a sight. Soot everywhere: counter, windows, table, and
chairs. My shoes made smeary footprints on the cement

floor. The worst thing was the smell. It burned my throat just to breathe. The deer head hung slightly crooked, its yellow antlers coated with soot. I pulled over a chair. Up close I could see the mouth had been sewn shut with thick thread. I poked the neck. I had expected it to be stuffed with foam rubber or some‐thing, but it was too hard. The eyes looked like cat's‐eye marbles up close. Patches of fur were missing from its face. I grabbed the head by its antlers and tried to pull it off the wall. My chair teetered a little and I held the head for dear life. I worked it back and forth until I felt something give. Though it now hung very crooked, it still wouldn't come loose.

"Dang it all," I shouted, giving a tug with all my might. It broke free and came tumbling toward my face. I twisted away and let it go. I felt my chair tip onto two legs. The deer head thunked to the cement a split second before I made a leap for safety. When I landed, I found myself sitting dangerously close to the antler points.

The head and I stared at each other. It had been attached to a wooden plaque that was still on the wall. When I turned the head over I could see into the neck. It was stuffed with something, definitely not foam rubber. It looked like a towel. I pulled it out and saw it was tied with a piece of twine. There was something wrapped inside. It had to be the money! I had trouble with the knots because my fingers had become thumbs and refused to cooperate. Finally, I undid the last of the knots and unfolded the towel.

A book. Not money, but a plain little book. It had a leather cover worn smooth like Gran's Bible. Some yellowed pages fell out when I flipped through it. My heart sank rock bottom. The book, whatever it was, sure wouldn't pay any medical bills. I sat for a minute, holding the stupid thing, wanting to throw it hard as I could against the wall. I looked at one of the pages and squinted at the faded writing. *Coltsfoot, mandrake, foxglove, peppermint . . . steep for three minutes . . . for the treatment of . . . a potion to stimulate . . .* Each page had a list of peculiar ingredients, mostly plants. The instructions reminded me of the way *Silas Marner* was written: strange. Not like any recipe in *The Joy of Cooking.*

I was at a dead end. Seemed like mysteries kept piling up like dirty laundry and I was fresh out of clues. I stuffed the loose pages back in the book. One of the papers was folded in half. It was pale green and had lines and didn't match the pages of the book. I unfolded it and almost screamed my brains out. It was another one of Ol' Man Hazard's mind-boggling riddles. It said:

If its hot in the kichen
Than turn down the hete.
Youl find the hid treasure
When you cook something sweat.

Give up Missy?

Missy? I could have slapped myself silly for being so thick. Missy *had* to be Ol' Lady Hazard. The riddle had to be to her. Who else would it be to? I thought about my weird visit with Ol' Lady Hazard, how she mentioned that she called Gran Sissy. Did they go by the rhyming names of Missy and Sissy? Was Gran actually *friends* with the town witch? And what did this book of crazy recipes have to do with a hidden treasure? Sure as heck, this was the thing that she had said Ol' Man Hazard had swiped from her, just out of meanness. This was what she had been digging for—not the money—that day the Tobster and I near wet our pants when we saw her. Maybe Ol' Man Hazard had hid it to protect himself from her. I needed to look it over some more and try to figure things out.

I stuffed the book inside my jacket and hurried back through Hazard Swamp.

"Momma? Gramps?" I hollered when I got home. The house was dead quiet. I took the steps two at a time. I hoped Momma would be coming home soon with good news that Gran was better. Maybe those antibiotics were working. I wondered about supper.

Gran had said she wanted me to bring Missy—Ol' Lady Hazard—to her. I was hoping the book would tell me why. After all, wasn't it Ol' Lady Hazard's tonic that had made Gran take a bad turn to begin with? Or was Gran already feeling bad when she went to Ol' Lady Hazard? Maybe Gran *thought* that this Missy person could fix her up. I was suspicious of the whole thing, and Gran was in too bad of shape to explain anything, or know what was best for her. I looked through the book, more careful this time. I decided to tuck Riddle Number Two into *Silas Marner* for safekeeping, along with my tattered book report that I'd salvaged from the Voodoo Shack.

I turned my attention back to the recipe book, hoping to find some answers. I'd never seen a book on witchcraft, and I almost expected to be struck dead for having it. I was a little disappointed, though, because the first few pages of the book listed a bunch of people, a lot of them with the last name of Horvath. That sounded mysterious and foreign. Maybe that was Ol' Lady Hazard's name once. There were dates written next to the names, like in Gran's Bible, probably showing when folks were born and when they had passed on.

Blanche Horvath, now Hazard–yep, that was her name before she got married–was born in 1898. Holy smokes, was she ever old! I did some calculating–sixty-four. Maybe around Gran's age. Ancient! Blanche Horvath married William Donald Hazard on October 7, 1917. I did some more calculating. She was nineteen when they were married. Next line down was indented. It said April 24, 1918, infant girl, stillborn. I pondered what stillborn meant. I supposed it meant born dead. I did some more calculating. The infant girl was born a little over six months after they married. But it took nine months to have a baby! I felt my cheeks tingle. Ol' Lady Hazard *had* to get married! Then the baby was born dead.

Alice Pruitt's name-calling from a few days ago poked at me. Illegitimate. It wasn't the same for Ol' Lady Hazard, though. She had been married when her baby was born. Best I could piece together, my father had died before I was even born. I shrugged my shoulders. At least I hadn't been stillborn!

I turned the pages carefully because they seemed to want to crumble in my fingers. I was getting into the good stuff now. It looked like maybe recipes for casting spells and such. When I looked closer, though, they seemed more like concoctions for what ails a body. I came to a page saying it was good for *women's miseries.* Another called for peppermint to settle a stomach. There were cures for headaches, heartaches, backaches, stomachaches, toothaches, and septic wounds, what-ever that meant. There was a treatment for something called *The Infantile.* Some of the recipes had a list of ingredients as long as a kid's Christmas list. I was just curious, mind you, when I set to looking for a potion geared to cure pneumonia. Couldn't hurt to look, I figured. If there was a magic cure for Gran, though, it didn't jump out at me.

I was getting to the end of the book when I stopped at a faded page. It had a recipe in it that said it was for the *Release of Sadness and Woe from the Soul.* It took two kinds of mushrooms and a bunch of other stuff. At the end of the recipe it said, *Hallucinogen if taken while imbibing of alcoholic drinks.* There was a word written at the bottom of the page that had much darker, newer-looking ink. It said *Bill.* I suspected it was Ol' Lady Hazard's writing, since Bill was her husband. I stared at the page for a minute, wondering if she had used that recipe on Ol' Man Hazard to release woe from the soul.

I pulled my dictionary over and started looking up words. *Woe:* grievous distress; an affliction. I found *hallucinate: To wander in mind . . . dream. Imbibe: To drink; to absorb as in a liquid; to receive into the mind.*

I was getting more confused by the minute. It had to be the drinking, liquid–absorbing imbibe, not the receiving into the mind. But to hallucinate was to have the mind wander, so maybe imbibing made the mind wander. But it didn't say that in the dictionary. I shook my head trying to clear the confusion. It could be a *hallucinogen* if taken while *imbibing* alcoholic beverages. So maybe Ol' Lady Hazard wrote her husband's name next to that recipe to remind her that his mind could wander if he took that potion while drinking alcohol, like the beer he always had in his hand.

But why would he take the potion? It wasn't something that came in a can like soup. From what Ol' Lady Hazard said that day I was held captive at her house, her husband didn't think much of her remedies. Maybe that's why he took the book and hid it. I expected he wouldn't dream of taking any of her potions, at least not on purpose.

I felt a tingle go up my scalp. I was sure if I looked in a mirror, I would find my hair standing straight up. What if he didn't know he was taking it because she snuck it in the meat loaf or something? Maybe she wanted to make him feel better because he was full of that *woe*. But she knew he drank beer most all the time, so why would she give him something that might make his mind wander, especially since he was always handling guns?

It seemed kind of far–fetched, still. And Gran was calling for "Missy," probably thinking she could help. I would do anything to help Gran, and the doctors seemed stumped. Maybe Ol' Lady Hazard could help

Gran; then again, maybe she would finish her off, like Ol' Man Hazard. There was no getting around the fact that the book belonged to Ol' Lady Hazard. All in all, I wondered if I shouldn't just turn the book over to her as the rightful owner. But what if she'd killed her husband, or at least got him doped up by sneaking him some of the potion for the soul? She would have known he'd be washing it down with a beer sooner or later. She had to know it would make him hallucinate. She knew it was near deer hunting season and that he would be cleaning his gun. If Ol' Lady Hazard gave him the potion, she had to know he might blow himself clean to kingdom come with his shotgun.

Was it murder? Should I tell Deputy Skinner, or at least Momma? If I didn't, then I supposed I'd be an accomplice. If I decided to rat on her, the whole thing was so far-fetched, I doubted anyone would believe me, recipe book or not. Momma and Gran always said I had an overactive imagination.

I heard some noises coming from downstairs and quickly slid the little book under my pillow.

"Iris, you up there?" Momma hollered. I heard her come up the steps.

"Yes, Momma," I said, jumping up, and ran to her. Momma's uniform was crumpled and her nurse's hat was gone. We hugged real tight.

"How's Gran?"

"She's still with us, honey. We're keeping her comfortable. Let's grab us a bite and go on to the hospital to see her. We're going to pick up a friend of Gran's who wants to pay a visit. I told her that she may not be awake, but she insisted. Anyway, I don't mind. After all, we owe her a debt of gratitude for looking after you when you nearly burned yourself up."

Ol' Lady Hazard! Momma was bringing *her*? I had barely escaped from her clutches with my life. Of course, I never told it that way to Momma. All I said was that she'd taken me back to her house and fed me some soup. I left out all the gruesome details because I fig-ured things were stirred up enough.

"Come on down as soon as you're cleaned up," Momma said, and slipped out the door.

There I stood, holding a *possible* witch's book that held a *possible* clue to a murder and a *possible* cure for Gran, or maybe none of the above, or all of the above. But it was there, that stupid recipe book, peeking out from under my pillow, about as easy to ignore as a spotted elephant. I had to make a decision pretty soon. I wanted to do the right thing. Trouble was, I couldn't see right or wrong in any of the choices.

After I washed up and brushed my hair, I tucked the little book into the waist of my pants. I wore my shirt out to cover it up. It felt hard and sharp against my ribs. Before the day was over, I would turn the book over to *somebody*.

Chapter Thirteen

———•———

Greenie and his pa, Deputy Skinner, were coming out of Gran's room when we arrived.

"Hey, Iris," Greenie said, and gave me a little squeeze.

I could feel the recipe book cut into my ribs and slip down a little in my waistband.

"What's that–" Greenie started to say until I jabbed him good with my elbow.

"Tell you later," I whispered, glancing at Deputy Skinner. Fortunately, he was busy yakking with Momma and Ol' Lady Hazard. I wondered what he would think if he knew he might be standing less than a foot from a killer, and that the evidence was sliding out of my waistband. I gave the book a little nudge back into place.

"What is *she* doing here?" Greenie said, jabbing a thumb at Ol' Lady Hazard. We both took a look at her. She was wearing a long purple skirt, green sweater, and tennis shoes, along with the usual assortment of jewelry. She had her hair in a discombobulated bun held somehow by a couple of pointed sticks.

"Well, come on, son," said Deputy Skinner. "Now, Carolyn, if there's anything, anything at all. Me and my boy haven't forgot all the kindness your mother had for us when my Lucille passed on."

"Thank you, Walter. We're coping fine for now," Momma said.

Ol' Lady Hazard, Momma, and I slipped into Gran's room. Gran's eyes were closed but her lips were moving. No words were coming out.

"Probably tuckered from so much company," Ol' Lady Hazard said.

I moved next to the bed and held Gran's hand. I intended to keep close by, in case Ol' Lady Hazard whipped out some bottle of poison and tried to force it down her. There was a tube going into each of Gran's arms now, and another tube came out the end of the covers and into a bottle on the floor. Gran's chest rose and fell in short little pumps.

I looked at Momma. She had changed from her crumpled uniform to a skirt and sweater. Her hair was pulled back into its usual ponytail, and she had put on some frosty pink lipstick. Her eyes were moist. She bit her lip and said, "Blanche is here, Mom, and Iris."

Gran moved her lips and tried to talk. She sounded kind of bubbly. "Missy—that you?"

Ol' Lady Hazard nodded and moved toward the bed, her jewelry clicking and clacking. I tried to wedge myself between Gran and her, but Momma put her hand on my shoulder and pulled me back.

I felt the recipe book slip and had to hike it up again.

"Come on, Iris, let them be for a while," Momma said, pulling on me.

"But, Momma . . ."

"Let's go find Gramps. He's probably sleeping in the lounge," she said, tugging harder.

"I gotta go to the bathroom. I'll be there in a minute."

"Okay, honey. You know where it is?"

I nodded. Momma slipped out of the room and I followed, keeping an eye on Ol' Lady Hazard. I moved into the hall and watched Momma turn the corner to the lounge. I slipped back into Gran's room and slunk behind a screen that I suppose they slipped alongside a patient's bed for privacy before their sponge bath or something.

I peeked around the screen and watched Ol' Lady Hazard settle herself into the chair. "Now then, Sissy, I think yer jist being lazy, having folks wait on you hand and foot." She kind of cackled after that. I couldn't see Gran, but I suspected she wasn't doing any laughing.

"Oh, Sissy, if Bill hadn't took my book, I'm sure I could put ya right. There's a good formula for breaking the fever and clearing the lungs, but you know I've got a memory like a sieve." She shifted a little in her chair, like it wasn't comfortable, and I jumped back behind the screen. "All I had was that confounded riddle, and then I went and lost that. No matter, though, couldn't make head nor tail of it."

I watched Ol' Lady Hazard as best I could through a break in the curtain.

"He was so cruel, Sissy. Doctor said it was a sickness. You know I tried to help him with a special remedy, but he wouldn't have no part. Found out and that's when my book disappeared. 'Course, I still had some of my last batch, like I tol' ya, and I slipped it in his cream of mushroom soup the day he died. The whole thing was eatin' at me, Sissy. I was grateful to unload on you. I think yer right. Jist 'cause I put a dab in his lunch doesn't make me responsible. It was probably the beer. Still." She sighed, and plucked at her skirt.

I put my hand on the recipe book still held in my waistband.

"He knew that book held the remedy for my spells. They're gettin' worse now without my medicine. I've tried to remember. . . ." She tapped her finger to her temple. "I can't get it right, for the life uh me. I could kick myself for not having more than one copy. I tried some of them pills the doctor give me. Threw 'em right up, I did. Now, how's somethin' s'posed to work if you can't keep it down?"

I heard Gran cough a little so I took a peek outside the screen, to make sure Ol' Lady Hazard wasn't choking her. But she was just sitting there, hands folded in her lap, not even looking at Gran.

"I should uh taken yer advice, Sissy, and left Bill. But I stuck with that man . . . then I caught him stepping out on me. "

She reached toward Gran and I made ready to leap from behind the screen and shout. But Ol' Lady Hazard only patted Gran on the arm, careful not to disturb the tubes.

"An' ya helped me through it all, Sissy. Helped me cope. And I haven't forgot the money you give me, though you had none to spare. Least I can do is give you a little pick–me–up tea once in a while. Guess you need more than that, though."

Was that what Gran had gotten that day I spied on Ol' Lady Hazard's house, tea? Plain old tea. They had called it tonic. It was slowly dawning on me that my Gran and Ol' Lady Hazard had some kind of friendship. Looked like they shared secrets and troubles, just like us kids. Maybe her potion did make her husband go off his rocker and do himself in. But even so, she didn't do it on purpose.

Just then, Ol' Lady Hazard kind of stiffened in her chair and her eyes rolled back in their sockets. It was one of her trances again! I jumped from behind the screen and stumbled toward Gran, wacking my shin good on the corner of the bed. That set me to hopping around the room, holding my shin. Well, naturally, my elastic waistband wasn't up to the job, and the little book slipped out, down my pant leg, out the cuff, then kind of skidded a little until it settled at Ol' Lady Hazard's feet. This happened at the very instant that she came out of her trance, eyelids fluttering. She looked at the book, looked at me, then snatched it up quick and hugged it to her.

"Praise the Lord!" she shrieked, which woke Gran enough to make her squeak out a noise.

It was plain as day. Somebody higher up had made the decision for me about what to do with that book. After all, if I was supposed to turn the book over to Deputy Skinner as evidence, then the thing should have fallen out when he was still around.

When people use the expression about somebody's face lighting up, they surely must be talking about how Ol' Lady Hazard looked at that moment. She jangled over to me and crunched me with a squeeze, filling me with her sweet, spicy smell.

"You found my remedy book, child. Wherever... No matter. I thought it was gone fer sure. Go find yer ma, kiddo, I need to get home and fix a brew."

Dr. Wringer said it was one of the fastest recoveries he had ever seen. It wasn't but a few hours after Ol' Lady Hazard had cradled Gran's head to help her sip the potion through a straw that we all noticed an improvement. Of course, Dr. Wringer thought Ol' Lady Hazard was helping Gran with a few sips of 7UP when he peeked into the room at the most inopportune time. Anybody who smelled that concoction would have known in a minute that it wasn't 7UP. It smelled more like the basement on a humid day than soda pop.

"Now suck hard, Sissy," Ol' Lady Hazard had said. Gran screwed up her face something awful and tried to push the straw out with her tongue.

"It's me: Missy. Drink up, ya old pill," Ol' Lady Hazard said. That seemed to do it, and Gran stopped fighting the straw, and sucked the potion up.

I could have stopped it at any time by just calling Momma or someone else who worked in the hospital. But I couldn't forget what Ol' Lady Hazard had said, about how thankful she was to Gran. They were friends, and friends don't feed each other poison drinks. Gran smacked her lips a little, held out her tongue, and made a face like she'd just sucked on a lemon. When she said "Land sakes, Missy, you trying to poison me?" it was the first hint I'd seen of the old Gran in a long time, and I knew I'd done the right thing.

Well, anyway, by the next morning Gran was breathing easier. I was having my morning visit with her, and she was asking about her hens. I was relieved that Mary Beth–the chicken that had stopped laying– had popped out what I expected to be a double yoker, though we hadn't broken it open yet. I was telling Gran about it when a nurse bustled in, her uniform crackling like it had been triple starched.

"How are *we* today?" said Nurse Starch.

Gran snorted. "You tell me, you're the nurse."

Nurse Starch smiled, but it was fake. She shook down a thermometer and stuck it in Gran's mouth, probably more to hush her up than anything. After a minute or so, Gran pulled the thermometer out of her mouth and squinted at it.

"Well, Nurse, you gonna read this and tell me if I still have a temperature?"

Nurse Starch snatched the thermometer from Gran and gave her a dirty look. "You'll have to discuss that with Doctor," said the nurse as she wrote something on Gran's clipboard. Then the nurse looked at me. "How old are you?"

"Thirteen," I fibbed.

The nurse sniffed and stalked out of the room.

"Humph," said Gran, watching the nurse bustle out. "I can't stand that: *Doctor* will be in to see you–let me check with *Doctor*. Doctor who? Why not *the* doctor? This place is driving me crazy. Don't know how your momma can be around all these people talking non–sense. What in blazes is wrong with plain English?"

I snickered. Gran was back.

When Momma stopped in later, Gran told her she was hungry. Since Gran would take nourishment, as Momma called it, they unhooked one of the tubes. Next, Dr. Wringer pranced into the room and announced that Gran's temperature was normal. After he moved his stethoscope around Gran's chest and listened to her breathing, he smiled and declared that her lungs were clearing up. Miraculous, he said, then went on and on about the antibiotics.

Within two days, Gran was fighting to come home and Dr. Wringer said something about the hospital staff threatening mutiny if he didn't release her. Gramps came in just as we were packing her things and Momma was trying to make Gran get in a wheelchair.

"I'm not helpless, Carolyn. Get that thing away from me," she snapped.

"Hospital rules, Mom. If you want to get out of here, sit your butt down," Momma said. I stifled a snicker.

Gramps did the honors of pushing Gran down the hall, while Momma and I carried her suitcase and all the flowers folks had sent. Gran's minister had stopped in to see her before she was released, and he claimed her miraculous recovery was due to the prayer circle he had organized. Seemed everybody wanted to take credit for Gran getting better: There were Dr. Wringer's antibiotics, Reverend Buckman's prayer circle, and Ol'

Lady Hazard's potion. Way I figured it, the cure was maybe a mixture of a lot of things. If I had to pick the strongest ingredient, I'd have to say it was something else entirely, and that was Gran's *belief* that Ol' Lady Hazard could make her right as rain. So I guess when folks are busy passing out prizes for Gran's recovery, they should give the blue ribbon to Gran herself.

Chapter Fourteen

"It's got to be buried somewhere here in the swamp," I said. I wiped the sweat off my forehead and swatted at a few bugs. It was the first really warm day of spring and everyone was getting hot and cranky as we trudged through the muck of Hazard Swamp. My feet were sweating up a storm inside my rubber boots.

"I certainly hope you don't propose to dig up this whole marsh, Iris. We've got to pin the spot down," the Tobster said. He stopped and leaned on his shovel.

"I ain't gonna dig at all, until we're darn sure it's the right spot," Greenie said, making little slits in the ground with his shovel.

"That makes two of us," Randy said.

Cecilia swatted at the no-see-ums. "I *hate* bugs. So when do I get my part of the money?"

I noticed that she had brought a little tiny shovel, like the kind Momma might use to plant flowers. I wondered how much digging it would hold up to. I myself had dragged along a pick-axe, good for serious digging.

"Haven't you listened to anything that's been going on, Cecilia?" I said.

"Well, yeah. There's a buried treasure and we get a reward if we find it. I'm gonna buy Barbie's Dream House."

The Tobster sighed and wiped his brow. "Don't you remember, Cecilia? We're each going to turn over our share to Iris's family, to help pay her grandmother's hospital bill."

"*All* of it?"

"Yeah! All of it," Greenie said.

"Let me see that poorly written riddle again, Iris," said the Tobster. I handed it to him.

He scowled at it and read aloud: "'If its hot in the kichen'—he left out the *t* in kitchen—'Than'—*than* instead of *then*—'turn down the hete'—he spelled heat wrong also—'Youl find the hid treasure'—there's plenty wrong with that phrase—'when you cook something sweat'—I suppose he means 'sweet.' Lastly, of course, asking if Missy gives up."

"Well, one thing's for sure, I'm definitely hot. Does that mean we're getting warmer?" Randy said. He was trying to balance the end of the shovel handle in the palm of his hand.

"Knock it off, Whip; you're gonna kill someone," Greenie snapped.

"Come on, you guys, think!" I said, wanting to paste them all with the business end of my pick-axe.

"Yes, Iris is correct. The sooner we figure this out, the sooner we can all go home," said the Tobster.

"My vote is that it has to be somewhere in the cabin," I said. "The other clue led me there."

Greenie stood. "Come on. Let's go. Maybe we'll see something we ain't caught before."

"Haven't caught," the Tobster corrected.

"Shut up," Greenie said.

"You shut up," the Tobster said, his face turning red.

"Both of you shut up," I said. "I'm getting a head–ache. We're never gonna be able to find the money at this rate. You guys promised."

The Tobster and Greenie studied the tops of their shoes for a while.

"Yeah, let's go. I'm getting all bitten up," the Tobster said, swatting at the back of his neck.

By the time we reached the Voodoo Shack, I had blisters on my heels from my rubber boots.

"Pu–wee," Greenie said, pinching his nose. The odor hadn't improved. If anything it smelled worse. We propped the door open to let in some fresh air. The tables and chairs were covered with soot, which we realized too late.

"Silas Marner hid his gold by digging a hole in the floor of his house," I said.

We all stared at the cement floor of the cabin.

"You don't think Ol' Man Hazard dug a hole, then cemented over it, do you?" the Tobster said.

"No way are we digging into this floor," Greenie said, clinking his shovel blade on the concrete.

"I know it's all here, in this riddle, if only I could figure it out," I said, waving the tattered piece of paper around.

"Maybe it's in code or something, like in the military," Greenie said.

The Tobster snorted.

I looked around the room, then looked at Riddle Number Two.

"Okay, guys, listen up. 'If its hot in the kichen . . .'"

"What kitchen?" Cecilia said in her kind of whiny voice.

"Yeah, what kitchen?" Randy repeated like we hadn't heard Cecilia, who was sitting two inches away. "All this place has is a countertop with a sink that had a bucket under it to catch water and a couple of old cupboards and that whatchamacallit stove-thing."

"Yeah, and we've been through all of them a million times and haven't found one red cent," Cecilia said.

"Maybe the next line will be better: 'than turn down the heat.'"

"And how can you turn down the heat in a place with no little dial on the wall to do it?"

Greenie was looking around the cabin. "No thermostat nowhere, no furnace to turn down. Jeez, Iris, I can't believe you spent the night here," he said. "I swear, if I'd known you didn't hightail out when the storm hit, I'd uh come looking for you."

The Tobster snorted.

"Anyway, then it goes: 'Youl find the hid treasure, when you cook something sweat.' Cook something sweat? Oh, yeah, he meant sweet . . . like pies, cake . . ."

"Hold on a sec, I think I'm getting an idea," Greenie said.

The Tobster snorted.

"Knock it off, Toad, " Greenie said.

"What?" the Tobster said, real innocent-like.

"I heard that sound you made, for the *third* time. I asked you what it's supposed to mean."

"I have trouble with my sinuses, okay? The air in here is bad," the Tobster said. He took out a little squeeze bottle and squirted spray into each nostril.

"Will you both just shut up!" I wailed.

Everyone stared at me like I was possessed by Satan himself. Everyone, that is, except Cecilia, who was staring at the door.

"Who invited *her*?" Cecilia said.

We all swiveled around to see Alice the Malice standing in the doorway, hands on her hips.

"What a dump!" Alice said in a pretty good imitation of Bette Davis.

"Do you reckon we should tie her up?" Randy asked.

We had all temporarily forgotten about finding the money, our attention being shifted to our captive. She was perched on the very edge of the mattress-less bunk bed, trying to stay clean. Her normally poofy hairdo was a mite deflated, probably because I'd accidentally crushed it with my elbow in the scuffle to catch her.

"You kids can't make me stay here. Kidnapping is against the law."

"So's trespassing—against the law. So I guess they'll lock you up, too—" I snapped.

"If they ever find her," Randy said.

"Yeah, *if* they ever find her," I said, playing along.

"Where's she going?" Cecilia said.

"You know, I heard a story once of how some psycho buried somebody in a coffin with a little air tube and kept them there until a ransom was paid," Randy said.

"Well, we do have lots of shovels . . ." I said.

"Or maybe cement shoes," Randy said, warming up to his stories.

"Huh?" Alice said, looking at her feet. She smoothed back a chunk of hair that kept falling in her face.

"You know, like the mobsters. They put someone's feet in cement and throw them off the bridge into a river," Randy said.

"Oh, there's a well-thought plan," the Tobster said. "And just where do you propose we find a bridge and a river, not to mention cement?"

Randy jutted out his chin. "Well, there's Thompson's Creek."

The Tobster snorted. "Yeah, that must be about six inches deep. I suppose we could dump her in there with her cement overshoes and hope she'd die of a chill."

"Will you guys knock this off?" Greenie said. "First, we ain't gonna kill nobody."

"Anybody," the Tobster corrected.

"Greenie's right," I said. "We've got to think of some way to shut Alice up . . . short of murder."

All the while Alice was looking from one of us to the other. She tried to smirk like she wasn't worried, but I could tell she was nervous because I caught her picking at a pimple on her forehead.

We all started talking at once, making far-fetched suggestions, like hypnotizing her. I wanted to get back to Riddle Number Two, get the cash, and pay Gran's hospital bill, but everyone was arguing.

"Excuse me!"

Our heads all cranked around at once to face Alice. We had forgotten about her for a minute, being caught up in our bickering.

"I have a suggestion," Alice said.

"Yeah?" Randy said.

"Yes. You could make me a member of your club."

We all gasped at once.

"I personally would rather eat worms and die," Randy said.

"Speak for yourself," Cecilia said.

I picked at some dirt under my fingernails and the Tobster brushed mud off his pants.

"Not that I am just *dying* to join–and I shall never set foot again in this cabin–however, I couldn't help but overhear your silly little riddle."

"You're not getting any of the money, and that's final!" I shouted.

Alice stood up and brushed off the seat of her pants. "I don't *need* money."

Like heck she didn't need money. I kept my vow of silence, though, and didn't mention the pawnshop incident. Randy was quiet about it, too, probably under the threat of death by his mother.

"If you'll allow me," she said, holding out her hand.

I just handed Riddle Number Two to her without thinking. She read it over, sighed, and stepped over to the countertop/sink/stove area. She started to pull open cupboards and drawers, holding the knobs gingerly, as if they were contagious. She peeked in the stove, under the sink, and in the cobwebby bucket. She pulled a nasty old canister off the counter. It had likely once had the word *sugar* on the side, but now all that was left were the letters U and G, spelling *ug*. Alice pried off the lid, which fell with a clatter. She inspected her fingernails for damage, then peered inside the canister.

"Humm," she said.

"We've looked in that thing. Nothing's there," Randy said.

"Honestly," Alice said, reaching inside and pulling something out. "It has a false bottom."

We all crowded over and looked into the canister. A hidden compartment! It looked too small to hold much money.

"Look out—is there anything in there?" I said, shoving the others away.

"There is something . . . if you'll . . . ouch!" Alice said, maybe feeling my elbow that accidentally jabbed her in the ribs.

There was something. It was another blasted piece of green lined paper! Another riddle!

I sat smack down on the hard, dirty floor, clutching that blasted piece of paper. Tobey gently pried my fingers from around it, unfolded it, and cleared his throat. "Well, it has the usual misspelled words. . . ."

"Just read it," I said.

"Do you like a good joke? This one comes with a hitch: you're thoroughly broke—and you're still a damn witch."

139

We all mulled it over for a while.

"So, it was just a stupid joke? There wasn't any money," I said, taking the paper back and looking at it, hoping for more clues.

"If there was, it ain't to be found," Greenie said.

"Isn't," Alice said.

"Not you, too!" Greenie said miserably.

"Well, anyway, people, that was a hoot," Alice said. "What's the next game? Can we leave this dreadful little hut?"

"There ain't no more games."

"Aren't," the Tobster corrected.

"That does it!" Greenie shouted.

It was all Randy and I could do to break up the two boys as they rolled and tumbled around on the soot-covered cement. They looked like a couple of winded coal miners when the fight ended. I could almost hear Mrs. Koklemeyer's shrieks of horror when she saw her Tobias's filthy clothes.

"I reckon this meeting is adjourned," I said.

Chapter Fifteen

On Saturday, two days before Easter vacation ended, Greenie Skinner called and asked how Gran was doing. When I told him she was champing at the bit, he asked if I wanted to go to the new movie showing at the Sun Theater, *The Haunted Mansion*. He added that the Tobster and Alice Pruitt were thinking about going along, too.

It was a first, Greenie asking me to a movie. And since when were Greenie and the Tobster buddies that they would plan this? The last time I saw them together, they were grunting and scrambling around on the dirty floor of the Voodoo Shack. Another surprise was that the Tobster and *Alice Pruitt* were going out together. I thought that the Tobster was, well, crazy about *me*. Maybe my not showing up that night when Momma sent me to the Koklemeyers hurt him bad. I guessed he had to look elsewhere for a girl. Not that I wanted to be his girl, or anybody's girl, for that matter.

When I asked Momma if I could go to the movies with Greenie, she told me to ask Gran. That made me feel good, knowing Gran was back in charge again. She was running things pretty much from her bed and was only supposed to get up to go to the bathroom. Of course, she didn't pay any mind to those orders, and Momma and Gramps had to shoo her out of the kitchen more than once.

When I walked into Gran's bedroom, I found her with snapshots scattered all over the bedspread and a big photo album opened on her lap. She had gotten a ton of flowers in the hospital and they now took up every inch of space on her dresser and windowsill. There were several bottles of medicine on her night-stand. A food tray sat on the chair next to her bed. Looked like she had eaten every scrap off it. Gran's hair was back up in its bun, and there was even a little patch of pink on each of her cheeks.

"I figure I'll make use of my time and put all these pictures in this album I got—when was it?—two Christ-mases ago."

She sorted through a stack of photos and cackled.

"Here's when you were just a little mite," she said, holding up a picture of me in a taffeta dress.

I had always hated that dress because it was scratchy. I'd eat worms and die before I'd tell Gran that, though, since she had sewn it herself.

I shifted my weight from one foot to the other and cleared my throat.

"What is it, Iris? I don't suppose you came in here just to view the scenery."

"Well, um, Greenie and me—I, mean, Greenie and I— that is, Greenie asked me to go to the movies."

I knew Greenie was not Gran's favorite person, so I added, "Along with Tobey Koklemeyer and Alice Pruitt."

"That so?" she said, and kept looking at photos.

"Yes 'um."

"What movie would it be you were hoping to see?"

"Something about a mansion, I think."

"Humpf. More likely that horror show that's playing."

"I don't think it's too scary."

"With that Skinner boy, huh?"

"Yes 'um."

She looked up from her pictures. "Walter Skinner gave me those nice posies over there. Mums. My favorite."

"They're real pretty," I said, feeling a glimmer of hope.

"I don't suppose it's been easy for the boy, growing up without his mother."

I shook my head, then nodded, trying to be agreeable.

"Course, I don't suppose it's any easier growing up without a father," she said.

I shrugged my shoulders. I wasn't sure what she was getting at.

Gran looked at a photograph for a moment, then shoved it across the bedspread toward me.

"Mighty handsome fellow, your father. No wonder your momma fell head over heels for him. Gramps says war does that to people."

I picked up the photograph and stared at the smiling couple. The woman was Momma, younger, her hair in its nurse-on-duty pageboy. She wore a uniform with a little tie at her neck and a goofy hat on her head. The uniform skirt came way below her knees. She was smiling up at the man next to her. He wore a uniform, too, with funny stripes on the sleeves. He was trim and tall with dark hair. He was looking at Momma, smiling at her. He looked familiar, though I'd never met him.

"That's the only picture your momma brought back of your father. She says it's the day he got promoted to sergeant. I can see you got some of his traits," Gran said. She peered at me over the tops of her wire-rimmed glasses. "Course, you're not handsome, men are handsome. But you do clean up to a comely young lady, if you've a mind."

I felt the tops of my ears heat up again.

"Your momma knows she should talk to you about your father, but it's real hard for her, Iris."

I nodded.

"See, she and your father were going to get married soon as they both could get a leave–time off from their duties. They had it all arranged to get hitched soon as he got back from a maneuver. Trouble was, he never came back."

"You mean that's when he was killed?" I asked.

"Yes, child. It nearly did your momma in. Her letters were so filled with sorrow and grief. I was worried sick, and so far away from her. Your gramps and I would have hopped a plane to Korea if we could have. Well, then she found out she was in the family way."

"You mean pregnant?" I asked. I remembered that was what Momma told me at the Tastee Treat.

Gran gave me a sharp look.

144

"In my day, we called it– Oh, never mind. Yes, Iris, you were on the way. I . . . well, I'm afraid we were kind of hard on your momma at first, so she got that job in Detroit after you were born, I guess to put some miles between us. We came to miss her terrible, and you, too. Seems she always had to work and never came for a visit. Why, we didn't see you but twice until you moved here. Didn't stop Gramps and me from thinkin' about our granddaughter, though. And your momma did send along pictures." She picked up a photo and mumbled, "Scruffy little dickens, weren't you?"

So Alice was right. I *was* illegitimate. My father went off and got killed before he and Momma got married. I spent a minute plucking at a thread in Gran's bedspread. Gran reached over and took my hand.

"Now, Iris, there's nothing for you to be ashamed of. I'll allow that your momma and your father put the cart before the horse, and I could make up a dozen excuses for both of them, but I'm not one for excuses. That's all in the past and what matters is that you know you didn't do anything wrong, Iris. You understand that?"

I nodded and Gran squeezed my hand.

"I know folks in this town have been waggling their tongues ever since your Momma came back to the farm towing you 'long side. It's none of their business, but it's human nature to gossip," Gran said.

She let go of my hand and lifted my chin so I was looking her in the eye.

"You know you keep your momma going–give her a reason to live. Another thing, just because you weren't planned doesn't mean you aren't wanted."

I realized I was still holding the photo of Momma and my father. I started to hand it back to Gran.

"No, Iris, you keep that."

I nodded and looked at my mother and father again. The picture told me a lot. Now I could see a face instead of a blur when I thought about my father. It didn't seem to matter so much, the illegitimate thing. I thought about Alice with her bouffant hairdo and pimply forehead. I remembered how her mother acted that day Momma and I were having a Coke at the Tastee Treat. I remembered thinking back then that I wouldn't have traded places with Alice for anything. I wasn't mad at Alice anymore for her name-calling. In fact, I felt sorry for her and was even willing to forgive her for butting in and breaking the code on Riddle Number Two.

Gran sighed real loud and said, "I'll be so dang glad to get out of this bed. It's making my fanny sore, lying here all day. I have a mind to whip back these covers and go to the movies tonight with you and that Skinner boy."

When Gran saw the expression on my face, she cackled like a hen.

"You say Tobey Koklemeyer and What's-Her-Face are going along, too?" Gran asked.

"Alice Pruitt. Yes 'um."

"Didn't know you and Alice Pruitt were chums."

"We're not, but–"

Gran didn't let me finish. "Did you get that blasted book report done for school on Monday?"

I nodded. I was ahead of the game for once. I knew enough to finish up my report on *Silas Marner* before asking Gran about the movie.

"That so?" Gran said, surprised. "Let's hear it, then."

I had a suspicion Gran would want proof of my book report, so I had brought it along–all six pages in my best handwriting and a full two pages longer than my teacher had required. I figured this might get me some extra credit. I hadn't planned on reading it out loud, though. Reading out loud always made my ears turn beet red.

"The whole thing?" I asked. "I can leave it here for you to read later." Truth was, I wasn't sure what Gran *or* my teacher would think of it. It wasn't your ordinary book report.

"Why don't you start off reading, and we'll see," Gran said.

I cleared my throat. "Well, here goes.

"At first when I read this book, *Silas Marner,* I couldn't make sense of it at all. For starters, the person who wrote this book, George Eliot, is not really a he but a she, and her name was really Mary Anne Stevens. I guess she thought folks wouldn't buy a book written by a woman. That stumped me some, then when I started reading *Silas Marner,* I got even more stumped. The book starts off being about Mr. Marner himself. Then on into the book, it stops being about Silas Marner and seems to be about a lot of other people, like Dunstan and Godfrey Cass. All of a sudden, it's like I don't know who's talking unless it is George Eliot herself. I start getting used to that and turn the page, and presto, we go back to Silas! This went on so much it made my head spin.

If I had lived in Silas Marner's day, I would probably have said the devil was behind it."

I looked at Gran to see how she was taking the
report in so far. She had put down the photos she had
been holding and was listening to me real close.

"It got me to asking myself, how am I supposed to
write a book report on this when the author can't
even make up her mind on who she's writing
about? Then a light bulb went on in my brain! *Silas
Marner* is not about any person so much, it's more
about how people are. You know, sometimes folks
are real nice. Other times they're snotty as all heck
and other times they can be downright mean. Once
I got through the gristle and down to the meat of
the story, things made some sense.

"For example, there was a lot of superstition in
Silas Marner's time, and there still is today. Just
because somebody is a little different, we act like
they got a third eye growing in their forehead or
something. The people in *Silas Marner* thought he
was maybe possessed by Satan because he had
these strange spells and became unconscious. Well,
maybe George Eliot didn't know what made Mr.
Marner act freaky but I think I do. It's called
epilepsy. Silas Marner also knew how to use plants
to make medicine. He always used them to help
people, but he was afraid of what folks would
think, like it was the work of the devil.

"There was another reason that Mr. Marner was treated like an oddball, and that was because he really didn't know his family. Squire Cass, a real important man in the town, knew his lineage. Trouble was, nobody much seemed to like each other in that family. Two of the sons, Dunstan and Godfrey, flat out hated each other. All the family talked about was money, and how to get it. A lot of *Silas Marner* is about money. Seems when there's trouble, it's because of money."

"Amen," Gran said.
I guess she liked that part.

"Mr. Marner's best friend stole some church money and pinned the crime on Silas. Mr. Marner was convicted of the crime in everybody's mind, without any real trial or anything. I've felt that way a time or two, and it's not a good feeling."

I took a peek at Gran. She had pinched her lips together, like she was trying to keep from saying something. I hurried on to the next line.

"Just to add insult to injury, the woman who was going to marry Mr. Marner left him and got married to the ex–best friend who stole the money. This sunk old Silas about as low as a body can go. He sat and worked at his loom all day and hoarded the money he earned. Every day he counted the money, but he never spent it. No wonder people thought he was nuts!

"Seems whenever there's a pot of gold around, it's just ripe for being snitched. Anyone reading the book could pretty much guess that Mr. Marner and his loot would have to part. It's not natural, sitting and counting money for no reason. Now if a body was saving for something, like a new bike–"

"Iris, honey, I think you've drifted a little," Gran said. "Yes 'um. Well, anyway . . .

"Can you guess who did it? It was that no–good Dunstan Cass! Silas about had a conniption fit when he found out his money was gone. But what re–placed the money was something money couldn't buy, and that was love. Not the falling–in–love type, but the family type. It came to him in the form of a little girl named Eppie. Come to find out, it doesn't matter whose blood runs through a person's veins. Fact of the matter is that bloodlines are for race–horses, not people. (So there to the la–de–da Daugh–ters of the American Revulsion or whatever.)"

I thought for sure Gran would tell me I got off the point again, but instead she let loose with a little snicker.

"Truth be known, family love has nothing to do with bloodlines, or who your father is, but more with being around when somebody needs you.

When good old Silas found this family love, he never gave his money another thought. Ask me, I think a person can have a real good family life and still have room left over for a little money, but Silas was an all or nothing kind of man."

I heard Gran give a little snort. I looked up, expecting her to scold for that last line.

"I got one more paragraph and the conclusion. Do I have to keep reading?" I said.

"Nope. I've heard enough," Gran said, nodding her head thoughtfully.

I didn't like the sound of that.

"You've done a real good job, Iris. I can tell you put a lot of hard work and thought into this book report."

That was a relief. Truth was, I *had* put more into this book report than any other school assignment I had ever done. In fact, I had torn up the few pages I wrote to begin with–the version that I went back to the Voodoo Shack for. It still makes me want to laugh and cry at the same time to think I spent the night in that nasty place all for nothing. I had thought it was a masterpiece–the first book report–but when I sat down to finish it up, I decided that it was all wrong. That's why I tore it up and started over.

"Just leave it on my nightstand and I'll read the rest. I expect you might have a couple of misspelled words, too," Gran said.

"I expect so," I said. "Um, Gran, about the movie?"

"The movie? Oh, I reckon it will be all right. No necking, though. They'll be plenty of time for that later."

She let loose with an evil-sounding cackle. I was beginning to wonder if that potion had done something to Gran.

I wondered how Alice could stand the smell of the Tobster's cologne. It was so strong it threw off the flavor of my butter popcorn. Several people who had sat near us in the theater had gotten up and moved to seats farther away, partly because of the stench and partly because they couldn't see over Alice's hairdo. That was fine with me since one lady who moved had had plenty of hair herself *and* a hat and I couldn't see over or around her. After she'd sneezed for the hundredth time, she turned around and gave *me* a dirty look, then snatched up her squawking kid and moved away. Good riddance!

But there sat Alice, all cozy against the Tobster, nibbling at the popcorn they were sharing. Personally, I like to have my own popcorn tub. Trying to share popcorn has led to more than one battle between Gramps and me. Nope, I wasn't taking any chances on that with Greenie. I'd bought my own jumbo buttercup. Greenie had offered to pay, but I wouldn't let him because, before you'd know it, he'd be expecting me to share. Besides, this wasn't a date, and I was perfectly capable of paying my own way with the three dollars Momma had given me.

The scariest part of the movie was when the hero of the show was going from room to room in this big haunted mansion looking for some lady who was flitting around in a chiffon dress. All the people in the movie had gotten gussied up because they had thought they were going to a formal dinner party, but it was really a trick and they were all trapped there. The hero, who was tall and handsome like my father, was searching for the chiffon–dress lady.

No, not that room, you idiot!

I admit I flinched and might have moved an inch or two closer to Greenie. He draped his arm over the back of my chair. I moved my popcorn farther down my lap, just in case.

The hero went down a big slide, like the old coal shoot at our house, and landed in a nasty–looking basement with cobwebs everywhere. Chiffon Lady was there and all the other dummies who had wandered off. Everyone, except for Chiffon Lady, was smudged with black soot like they'd spent some time at the Voodoo Shack after the fire.

I shivered, thinking about my night there. I guess Greenie thought I was scared by the movie, and moved his hand to my shoulder. It felt okay.

I thought about Ol' Lady Hazard. Had the potion for his *woe* done Ol' Man Hazard in? I guessed I'd never know for sure. One thing I had come to understand, though, was why Ol' Lady Hazard had those spells. Gran told me that Ol' Lady Hazard had a disease called epilepsy that made her prone to seizures. So when I saw her go into those trances and her eyeballs rolled back into her head, it was something gone a little hay-wire in the brain. That was why she always rode a bicycle, because it was too dangerous to drive a car. She could take pills for the epilepsy, but she had come up with a medicine of her own. When she got the recipe book back, she was able to start making her concoction again. It was the same thing that Silas Marner had, and folks had thought he was possessed by the devil. I felt a little ashamed of myself, thinking she was some kind of a witch, but who could blame me? She dressed like she was blind and collected more junk than a pack rat. Who wouldn't think she was off her rocker? Eccentric, Gran called it.

The hero of the movie, who really did look like my father, burnt his fingers on a match he had lit to check out the basement. He shook it out and it was semi-dark again. Chiffon Lady was sniveling in the corner. I was glad Momma wasn't like Chiffon Lady, all helpless and weak. I found women like Chiffon Lady very tiresome. If Momma were in the movie, she would be helping to find their way out, not sitting in the corner, fretting.

One man tried to crawl back up the coal shoot, but slid back. His fancy suit was all messed up and his bow tie had come undone. I noticed that Chiffon Lady stayed surprisingly clean and tidy, and she must have used a whole can of hair spray because her hair still looked perfect. I thought about Momma, either wearing her nurse's pageboy hairdo or her ponytail when she was off duty. I reached up to my own hair. Momma and I had put in a few rollers earlier, and I expected it didn't look too bad. I didn't take to ratting it all up and spraying it.

My Hero was working a stone loose in the basement wall about the time another "guest" came shrieking down the coal shoot. Luckily, the new addition to the basement group just happened to be carrying a flash-light, which helped My Hero a lot in his stone removal. Other men had joined in, grunting and straining, pulling stones out of the basement wall. The ladies sat around and fretted. If it were me, I would be over there clawing those stones out of the wall, chiffon dress or not.

"I see a tunnel!" yelled the man holding the flash-light.

Strange. I was leaning against Greenie and his arm was snug around me. Even stranger, I hadn't eaten much of my popcorn.

Two more guests came down the shoot. That was it: everybody was there in the basement. My Hero was crawling through the hole in the wall.

"Johnnie, please be careful!" said Chiffon Lady, clutching her hands together.

My Hero told the others to follow, and they all traipsed through a tunnel that somehow led to free-dom outside the mansion walls. I held back a yawn. I was waiting for everybody to remember that they were out in the middle of nowhere and their cars were *inside* the mansion walls. They all stared at the man-sion. One guy said they should burn it down. But My Hero said no, that sometimes we had to live with things we couldn't explain, that we didn't have a right to destroy that which we didn't understand and feared.

They all turned and looked again at the mansion. The wind was whipping Chiffon Lady's dress around, but her hair still didn't move. My Hero grabbed her.

They hugged then kissed as a black circle on the screen closed around them. The spooky music got louder and names swirled across the screen.

The lights came on in the theater. I stood and stretched. Greenie was shaking his arm that had been around me.

"Guess my arm fell asleep," he said.

I held out my popcorn bucket to share. Better late than never. I decided then and there to take My Hero's advice and let be those things I didn't understand. It was an act of fate that put the recipe book back in Ol' Lady Hazard's hands, that was a fact. Another fact: I would have rather eaten worms and died than accuse Ol' Lady Hazard of any wrongdoing as long as Gran was around.

We tried to lose the Tobster and Alice in the crowd, but his cologne kept finding us. There wasn't anything more to do except stop by the Tastee Treat for an ice-cream soda.

The final mystery was still pecking at me some. That was whether or not Ol' Man Hazard stole that money. I had tried so hard to find it, first to buy me a new bike, then to bribe Ol' Lady Hazard, and finally to pay off Gran's hospital bill. After all my fussing, I found out that there was insurance to cover most of the hospital bill. Dr. Wringer told Momma that he wouldn't be sending a bill, and when Momma had a hissy, he told her that he had learned a lot from Gran's case, and that his career would be boosted by his publication in that medical magazine. So turned out I didn't need the money at all, except maybe for the new bike.

We all ordered chocolate sodas at the Tastee Treat. I was tempted to tell Alice that it would make her face break out worse, but I held back. It would have felt good to get in a lick or two, since she had spent a good amount of time discussing my "dreadful" clothes, my "horrid" hair, my "disgraceful" fingernails, and my "ridiculous" shoes. I kept telling myself that it was all a front, because she knew she was no better than me or anybody else, like Momma said. She knew it especially since they had put up a for-sale sign in front of her house.

Money sure made some folks squirrelly. That brought my mind back to the stolen money and where it was hidden. It was still itching at me something fierce. Of course, Ol' Man Hazard might have spent it all— assuming he *did* steal it—on carousing, boozing it up, and buying guns and such. Two thousand dollars was a lot to spend, though. I knew it was still out there, somewhere. I felt it in my bones. It was a family trait, Gran said, the Weston women feeling things in our bones. I could feel mine jumping a little, making me squirm. Gran once said that the Weston women's bones wouldn't rest until we put things right—right as rain.

Best Books '06